Praise for
JADINE

"Jadine Tomecelli is a complicated, seductive character in this unsparing look at the wages of abandonment in childhood. Veazey sets up tensions and their consequences in evocative prose interspersed with vivid scenes of deadly acts of violence. *Jadine* is a nuanced study in moral ambiguity in this unnerving story of a life imploding, developing relentlessly in power and resonance, propelling you to an ending that is wrenching and unforgettable."

Robert Henderson, *Boston Book Club*

"*Jadine* is a poignant tale of hope and despair, of a girl drifting through time in a reality all her own, grasping for something to hold onto. The hard facts of her life mock our most cherished American ideals: family, community, opportunity; and when the expectation for justice sours, the playing rules of life become frightening and something altogether different."

Barbara DeWall, *Arizona Review*

"Following a series of heartbreaking events and dealing with more tragedy than she can handle, Jadine transforms herself into Jade, even as bad luck follows her like a storm cloud. Jade's longing for approval and love is scorching and sad, and Veazey keeps the reader hoping until the very end for her salvation."

Benjamin Hoyt, *Literary Reviews*

"*Jadine* is a true account of Jadine Tomecelli whose traumas early in life fracture her ability to trust herself and others in this psychological drama. Her fate intertwines with Native American Billy-John as the two orphans struggle against their past. Visual moments of passion and rage, both graphic and poetic, propel you to an ending you will never forget, or forgive."

Wendy Shapiro, *Tampa Book Club*

JADINE

a novel by **Julie Bigg Veazey**

author of *Silent Cry* and *Reckless Indifference*

CreateSpace, Charleston, SC

Jadine was inspired by a true story.
Names and locations have been changed
to protect the privacy of the persons involved.

ISBN: 10-1451597770
ISBN-13: 9781451597776
Library of Congress Control Number: 2010905125

To contact the author by e-mail: jbiggvz@hotmail.com

CreateSpace, Charleston, SC
Printed in the United States of America

Acknowledgements:

Deep gratitude and thanks go to:

My early readers—Bill, Shary, Stevie and Lynn, the ultimate sharp-eyers.

Mary Linn Roby for her incisive skill in polishing Jadine by in-depth suggestions and judicious editing, and Karen Propp for her initial advice and guidance—both with sensitivity, dedication, and professionalism.

The Dover Children's Home, Dover, NH, formerly a home for orphans, in recognition of their current work with children in crisis.

My family for their constant support, individually and collectively, who transform and enrich every day of my life.

And to my cat, Lahey, who faithfully watches and waits.

To Bill,
my first reader and erudite critic, my partner in life, and in
all our adventures; because he believes in me,
everything is possible.

"None of us can help the things life has done to us. They're done before you realize it, and once they're done they make you do other things until at last everything comes between you and what you'd like to be, and you've lost your true self forever."

— Eugene O'Neill (*Long Day's Journey into Night*)

CHAPTER ONE

On a glorious fall day in October, when the leaves were at the height of color and Jadine was twelve, her mother, still with her apron on and with her navy blue LL Bean purse hanging from her arm, walked out of their cozy little cape on North Main Street for the last time. Jadine was in her seventh grade classroom, adding up columns of numbers, trying to come up with the correct sum, while, according to those who saw her, Lisa Tomecelli walked all the way to the bus station in downtown Dover and waited on a bench across the street from the Fish Shanty Restaurant for the 2:15 bus to Boston.

When Jadine came home from school, she scoured the house, looking for a note or some kind of explanation, but even after three days, still no word.

From her secret place behind the foliage of the purple smoke tree that Mama had planted when she was born, Jadine placed her hands over her ears to block out the sound of Papa angrily calling for her to come into the house. Years before, Mama had taught her a "grownup" word—*retreat*—and beneath this tree was their special spot that even Papa didn't know about. When daytime dissolved into soft tones of diffused light in which objects had no edges, this was where Jadine could pretend that it was Mama calling to her. It was almost dark when she entered the house through the side door.

No longer did her bedroom promise the happiness of Mama lying next to her, reading a chapter from a book she had brought home from the school library. Shivering at the thought, Jadine wondered if, that night before she left, Mama had stood over her as she lay sleeping. *If so, had it make her hesitate—even for a moment?* Pulling the pink and soft-green chenille coverlet over her head, she sobbed silently, frightened and alone.

Weeks ago, Jadine remembered overhearing loud voices and how she'd climbed out of bed to listen outside her parents' bedroom door.

"Where did you go last night?" Papa had sounded really angry.

"What do you care," Mama had answered in a low, defiant tone.

"Because you were drunk."

"It's an escape," she had said with a harsh laugh.

"From me?"

"Yes, you, and this whole boring life." Jadine had then heard a loud thwack that sounded like a hairbrush hitting the glass-top dressing table.

"You haven't touched me in months," Mama had added.

"I can't stand the smell of booze on you, Lisa. Besides, I've been out straight at work."

"Well, I can't take it anymore."

But, that must have been a dream, Jadine told herself, because her parents didn't get angry at each other.

And Mama didn't get drunk. As a matter of fact, her breath always smelled fresh, like Listerine. And when Jadine came home from school, that was the time she was the most fun, laughing and hiding in their retreat, not like mornings when Mama seemed sad and a little cranky. At times like that, she'd push Jadine away when she tried to get close, saying, "You're a big girl now. You don't need me. No one does." And then she'd pour herself black coffee and she'd stand by the back door, staring blankly into the yard.

No matter how hard she tried, Jadine could not imagine that Mama really believed that she didn't need her to read with her at night, to do her hair, to bake a birthday cake, to *be* there when she got home from school. And what about boys? Who was going to tell her how to feel about boys? Maybe Mama had thought that she was so unlovable she didn't want to spend one more day with her. Or even say goodbye.

After a few days, Jadine found herself wondering if she hadn't known all along that Mama would leave. Or maybe she had actually seen her hurry past the school. But it could also be that she never had any warning at all, no psychic sense of loss heading her way. Probably she was just telling herself a story, arranging what had happened, this way and that, until she could dream of a happy ending.

With Mama gone, no one would ever say "I love you" without Jadine believing that the sentence was a prelude to a farewell, an abandonment, a kick in the teeth.

The following week, there was a letter in the mailbox from Mama addressed to Raymond and Jadine Tomecelli. She held it to her face, breathing in deeply through her nose, hoping to capture some hint of Mama's scent. Assuming that Papa would be angry if she opened it without him being there, she tucked it inside her blouse, hardly able to wait for him to read it aloud, to tell her when Mama would be coming home. The envelope scratched her chest, but she hoped that placing it over her heart would mean that the letter inside contained good news. When she bounded out of the house to greet him in the driveway, Papa seemed amused when she handed him the letter—almost as though he was laughing at her.

"Well, now," he said, "let's see what your mother has to say for herself."

When he looked down at the letter, Jadine noticed that he had the beginning of a double chin, and for the first time realized that perhaps he was not the handsome man she had once thought he was.

"I just want to know when she'll be back," Jadine told him. She could feel an expectant flush spreading across her cheeks.

But, as Papa read aloud, Jadine's heart sank. Mama wrote that she had gone to Canada to take care of *her* mother, Grandma Jones, a relative that Jadine had never met. Or even heard of, for that matter. Actually, she thought Mama had told her that her parents had died soon after she had left home when she was seventeen. And, was her home . . . Canada? Is that where Mama had told her she grew up? It was all so confusing.

Even though they had never gone to church as a family, and Jadine didn't know much about God, every night since Mama left, she had a sense that she might be able to ask out loud, in the quiet of her little bedroom, for *someone* to help make Mama come back—explain to her how much she was missed. Someone or something larger than herself or Papa. She vowed that she'd never be naughty again. Never. She would get up in the morning the first time she was called, dry the dishes without being asked, sweep the floor, pick up after herself, never whine or talk back, say please and thank you, go to bed on time . . . anything Mama wanted.

In the letter, Mama had said she missed them both and that she hoped to return soon. How long is soon, Jadine wanted to know? Two more letters came over the next month and Jadine, still hopeful, cuddled up to Papa on the worn chocolate-brown velvet couch in the living room, listening intently as he read each word. One thing was odd, however. They never seemed like the sort of things that Mama would ever say.

CHAPTER TWO

How rudderless her life had become since Mama left, Jadine realized. Now she felt scared of everything, the quiet country road with no streetlights, the silence that stretched across the unlit yard beyond the garage and wound its way under the front door and spiraled through the house. Their house, where Mama had been the sunshine, was cold and spooky now. Before, when Jadine had returned home from school, she was never sure whether she'd find her mother asleep on the couch or in an excited mood. "Who cares about cleaning," she would cry on one of her "up" days, as she tuned the radio to a music station. Papa was always complaining about how messy the house was, but Jadine didn't care. It was just so much fun . . . Mama with her special lemonade and Jadine with a soda, dancing around the kitchen until they dropped to the floor with laughter.

Now, Papa said she was a big girl and didn't need someone to babysit her. Of course she didn't need someone to watch over her, but Jadine hated the hours that she had to spend alone after school, waiting for him to come home from the print shop. The first thing he always used to say as he walked in the door was how beat he felt, then he'd go to the sink and scrub the ink from his hands while Mama would whisper, "What a drag." Now, he still said it even though Mama wasn't there to hear him.

Outside, the weather had become damp and gray, edging toward snow, and yet, Papa didn't turn on the heat or even start a fire in the fireplace in the kitchen where they always ate now, since it was just the two of them. No more delicious smells of chicken roasting in the oven or burgers sizzling under the broiler. Just miserable meals of scrambled eggs or frozen pizza or macaroni and cheese—whatever Papa threw together when he got home from work, the same things over and over until she wanted to stick her finger down her throat, or scrape the food into the toilet when he wasn't looking. Although that was a laugh, because Jadine knew that she could have made faces at him or peed on the floor, and he wouldn't have noticed.

Papa was no fun at all now. Or perhaps he'd always been like that. She'd used to think of him as handsome, in an odd sort of way, but now, she noticed that his eyes were a little too close together, and his nose was swollen with broken capillaries like tiny spider webs. To avoid the loneliness of the house, she hid in the retreat behind the barn every afternoon, where the leaves had fallen and the shadows were rapidly lengthening. The sharp metallic scent of winter was in the air. Not that she needed to hide; no one was looking for her or gave a damn what she was doing. She could eat lots of candy or watch sexy shows on TV or throw her homework in the garbage, or even yell swears at the top of her lungs and no one would care.

One dreary afternoon, when it was nearly time for Papa to come home, Jadine went into the sitting room where the November sun shone thinly against the wallpaper, flowered with lilacs, and across the pumpkin pine floor. Beside her favorite rocker, Mama had stored the sweater she had been knitting. It had a royal blue background with a row of white snowflakes across the front and back. "You'll have to act surprised on Christmas morning," she had said many times and Jadine had promised to do so.

Holding the sweater up against her chest, Jadine stretched the one arm that had been completed out to the side. She had been so eager for Mama to finish it, but now, it felt itchy and was ugly. Slumping to the floor, she slowly pulled the needles out of their stitches, remembering how mad Mama used to get when she had made a mistake, angrily ripping out the stitches even though the flaw would never have been noticeable. Like her mother, Jadine pulled on the wool, hand over hand, until what had once been a half-knitted sweater became merely a pile of crinkled yarn that looked just like Jadine's hair after Mama took out her braids.

The following week, Papa called Jadine into the bathroom. Wielding a pair of scissors, he told her to sit on the toilet seat as he picked up one of her braids.

"What are you going to do?" Jadine jerked her head back, but he didn't let go of the braid. "No, Papa, please don't. Mama wouldn't want you to."

"Your mama doesn't give a damn about you. Or me, for that matter. If she did, she'd be here. Now hold still."

But either the scissors weren't sharp enough or the braids were too fat, because he kept hacking away at them, ignoring Jadine's sobs which turned to hysterical screams when, after the braids came off, he continued to snip away at what was left of her hair.

"I hate you, Papa," she cried over and over again. "I hate you, and Mama does, too."

"Quit acting like a baby," he told her. "I don't do braids, and your mother's not here to coddle you."

"When Mama comes home, she'll be really mad at what you did to me, and I will *never* forgive you." When Jadine pulled at the roll of toilet paper to wipe her eyes, his hand shot out and broke it off at three sheets. She noticed the black printer's ink under his nails, and recoiled.

"You may as well get used to the fact that your mother is not coming home—ever," he said. "And there will be no more letters from her."

"How do you know that?" Jadine demanded, hating him.

"Believe me, I know," he muttered to himself. "I want you to get upstairs right now and go to bed." With that, he wiped the scissors on his pants, locked them closed, and left the bathroom.

Lying in bed that same night, Jadine guessed that maybe she wasn't just sad because of what he'd done to her, that he didn't care what she looked like, or how the kids at school would laugh at her. Maybe she really felt this way because he couldn't understand how alone and scared she was.

Looking back, Jadine realized that she had not imagined the trouble between her parents. In fact, even before her mother had left, Jadine had been haunted by the fear of being abandoned, a fear which, at the time, she had not been able to explain. But, along with that cold awfulness of it was a weird relief, too, because what Jadine had always known without knowing she knew had finally happened. No longer did she feel her stomach tighten when she walked past her parents' closed door at night. No longer did she have to try extra hard to drive away Mama's sadness. No longer did she have to fear the house rocking with her parents' anger—now, there was only her own.

Jadine fantasized about running away to punish Papa, but knew she was too scared to do it. Instead, she pictured Mama, delicate and pretty, putting on her makeup, leaning over the bathroom counter, getting closer to the mirror so she could draw in her eyebrows and put on lipstick before suddenly locking eyes with her daughter in the mirror and making a funny face.

The next morning, Jadine retrieved the shorn braids from the bathroom wastebasket and wrapped them in Mama's favorite scarf, the deep purple one with gold swirls like the sky on a windy day. Placing them in a shoebox, and then a plastic bag, she hid it in her retreat under pine boughs she had gathered in the woods.

Mama had left almost everything behind, and whenever Jadine stood in her parents' closet and pressed her face against the soft dresses that still smelled faintly of tobacco, Jadine could hear Mama's low throaty laugh. She even put her nose inside the shoes Mama wore around the house, the heels of which were worn down to almost nothing. She found her watch on the nightstand and put it on, pushing the expandable band up her arm until it held.

The kitchen curtains, the bathroom wallpaper, the painted frame of the mirror over her dressing table, even a wastebasket she had brought home, excitedly, from a yard sale were all in Mama's favorite colors, lavender and purple. Sometimes Jadine felt that those colors would smother her. In each drawer she opened, she seemed to learn something new about her mother. Once she found a photo of Papa where his face had jagged slashes cut across it, and a faded certificate from 4H saying Mama, at twelve, had canned the best jelly in her group—the same age as Jadine now. With each new discovery, her absence became more of a mystery.

In a dream one night, wearing a dress that Jadine didn't recognize, cut from a fabric so lovely and lustrous that it shone, Mama came to her in their retreat. Surprised and happy, she held out her arms, but Mama had laughed really loudly and pushed her away. "Your hair looks ugly," she'd said. "What in heaven's name did you do to it?"

Waking suddenly, trembling, Jadine imagined her own funeral at which her mother wept inconsolably.

CHAPTER THREE

When Thanksgiving, which had been Mama's favorite holiday, came and went, there had been no smell of turkey and apple pie baking in the oven at the Tomecelli house, no walk through the woods, crisp with frost, to build their appetites— just two frozen dinners of leathery turkey floating in a gross gravy and a few limp carrots, while Papa read the newspaper. Having hoped to please him, Jadine had put the plastic turkey with the bobbing head and some colorful maple leaves on the table.

After the meal, he'd said, "Get rid of that junk."

The week after Thanksgiving, Papa hired Claire Beckwith to be a live-in housekeeper; her daughter, Angie, was four years younger than Jadine. Actually, that was the same time that Mama's three letters disappeared from her bureau drawer. *So what?* Mama didn't care about her, so why should she care about those letters that never said she was sorry, never asked for forgiveness, never asked how she was doing? Besides, maybe Mama hadn't written them. Perhaps Papa had . . . to make himself feel better.

She had been so sure, at first, that someone *must* have made her mother leave, that Mama hadn't had a choice—that she surely missed Jadine so much that she cried for her all the time. Without realizing their value, Jadine's dreams filled her nights with someone calling her name in her mother's voice that rose from silence like an echo caught in the folds of sleep.

And then she began to wonder if Mama might be dead.

In the beginning, the housekeeper's warmth felt seductive, and Jadine was drawn to the tenderness she showed to her own daughter, Angie. She kept hoping that *she* would become part of that circle of love; a circle that didn't take her long to understand would never open wide enough to include her, especially when Papa *wasn't* around.

She even took over Mama's platform rocker like it was hers—the one Mama had rocked Jadine in when she was a baby.

At school, the kids were making Christmas gifts for their mothers from different items the teacher had spread out on the work table—buttons, silver and gold sparkles, pipe cleaners, ribbons, plastic stones that looked like gems, all colors—everything to decorate the little jewelry boxes that they had folded and glued together from cardboard. Jadine chose a purple marker and wrote *mother* on all four sides of her box. She stared out the window as the sun went bleak and pallid toward the woods; the fringes of the afternoon had already crossed into shadow. Using a black marker, she wrote Jadine on the top of her box and immediately scribbled all over it, blanking out her name. Realizing her teacher would be disappointed if she saw it, she made a fat bow out of purple grosgrain ribbon and glued it to the top.

On the way home, not caring at all who might see her, Jadine threw the box to the ground and stomped on it before leaving it by the side of the road.

✳ ✳ ✳

Mrs. Beckwith was a large-boned woman in her early forties with perpetually rosy cheeks, and when she was angry, her lips thinned. She was so unlike Jadine's mother, who almost never yelled. One time when she had, Jadine had been drawing at the kitchen table and her magic marker had slid off the paper, leaving indelible streaks on the tabletop. But after scolding her, Mama ended up saying that some day, when Jadine was grown up, she would look at those marks and be happy they were there. And Mama had hugged her and said she was sorry for getting mad.

No way did this ever happen with Beaknose, a name Jadine had decided to call Mrs. Beckwith, although, of course, not out loud. When *she* yelled, it was like she had a built-in megaphone: "JAYDEEEN, will you, for heaven's sake, get yourself back into the bathroom and clean it this time like I showed you?"

"Ray, can't you do something with that child?" she heard Beaknose complain to Papa later that same evening. "She is such a klutz, always spilling her milk or bumping into things. And sullen. Not a good role model for Angie."

Ennie, meanie, miney, moe . . . out goes Y O U. This jingle beat through her mind every time Beaknose ignored her, as usual, or gave Angie first choice on *everything.* Angie, her adorable sweet new "sister", with golden curls and blue, blue eyes…blue eyes that, ironically enough, shone with admiration whenever Jadine entered the room. Because Jadine was older. Taller. Ahead of Angie at school. Without meaning to, Jadine enjoyed the younger girl's attention. *Besides, Angie couldn't really be blamed for her mother acting so mean.*

But, it didn't take long for a mysterious sense of danger to set in, as though something was caught in her throat. Her defenses multiplied, and she clung to her dreams more tightly than ever, even as she was being drawn into her father's new life. During their cuddle times, Jadine no longer hovered by Beaknose and Angie, hoping to be included. Instead, she'd stand in the little half-bath on the first floor where the walls were covered with a tiny print of lilac, even on the ceiling, flushing the toilet again and again, not caring if it overflowed— anything to make Beaknose notice her. All the while, she continued to hold the memory of her beautiful mother, who had walked away and discarded her like a candy wrapper.

✧ ✧ ✧

One ordinary day in the second week in January, while Jadine and Angie were in school, Beaknose moved her things from the guest room to Papa's bedroom. Nobody asked *her* if it was okay. Nobody asked *Jadine* if it was all right for Mama's books, her rings and necklaces, and the purple dressing gown that still held a faint, faint scent of her to disappear. But they all did.

When she asked where Mama's things had gone, Papa said: "It's time to be done with all that."

Even more unpalatable, overnight, Mrs. Beckwith was to be called "Mama Claire."

Jadine, now fully deposed as an only child, spent as much time as she could out of the house, learning to rely on herself. Her stepmother was not a mother to her, always hanging all over Papa, who didn't even smell the same. He had the smell of "Mama Claire", starchy and uninviting.

But the worst part of all this was that Jadine was losing the ability to conjure up the sound of Mama's laughter, or the touch of her hand.

One Sunday dinner in early March, Papa asked everyone to hold hands around the table. Jadine thought it was because Beaknose was going to say another one of those before-you-eat prayers, but instead, Papa, with a huge stupid grin, looking straight at her, announced that he was going to marry "Mama Claire," and that he had sold the house because they were moving to Rochester, only a few miles north of Dover. He said it almost casually, all in one breath, adding with a wink that Rochester was called the Lilac City. Jadine wanted to swear and throw her plate at Papa and tell him how much she hated him. She wanted to scratch that triumphant smile off Beaknose's face.

After everyone was asleep that night, Jadine, heart racing, took a large plastic bag and a flashlight from the kitchen drawer and tiptoed out of the house to her retreat. Uncovering the box that held her braids and all the reminders of Mama that she had hidden there, including the dozen or so leaves from the purple smoke tree she had pressed last fall, she placed it in the dry bag. Streaks of moonlight filtered through the barren branches of the tree as, returning to the house, she followed her trail of footsteps in the rain-laden ground which sparkled with a dancing blue glow.

She would, she promised herself, make a new retreat. Wherever Papa made her go, she would have her own secret place, a place to which she could escape this new reality she hated so.

CHAPTER FOUR

After Papa "married" Beaknose, something Jadine realized years later that he couldn't have done legally because he had never divorced Mama, the family moved to Rochester, into the farmhouse that Beaknose had inherited from her grandparents.

By now, six months had passed and Jadine was having trouble picturing Mama, remembering the details of Mama's face, and she could no longer depend on photos since Papa, damn him—damn him to hell—had thrown out anything to do with their former life when they moved.

But she remembered the idea of her. And that was something he could never take away from her.

✵ ✵ ✵

Rochester was a small city with the requisite police station, town hall, and library, all clustered together. The old farmhouse was located on the outskirts of the town, set back from the road, with a long driveway lined on both sides with mature oak trees. Inside, the rooms were small and invitingly old-fashioned. And there was no purple anything, anywhere, except for lilacs growing by the side porch which Jadine didn't want to look at. When they bloomed next spring, she told herself, she would hold her breath to block their pungent smell.

She had already created a new retreat behind the shed that had been used to store equipment when the farm was operational. It was a perfect hiding place. Beaknose had told the children not to go near it because it was ready to fall down, and Angie, a silly goody-good, never did anything she wasn't supposed to, except when she copied her big sister. There, Jadine had safely hidden her retreat box that held her braids, wrapped in Mama's scarf, leaves from the purple smoke tree, Mama's hairbrush with her curly brown hair still in it, Mama's knitting needles, and a silver chain with a heart-shaped locket that she had found behind the bureau when they moved. Her heart had jumped when she first found it. She had held her breath before opening it, hoping that her Mama's picture would be there. But it was empty.

Close to the shed and her new retreat was the barn, so much bigger than the house, and her next favorite place. Jadine liked to lure Angie into its dark interior, hiding from her in the loft when she yelled her name. The old hay made her skin itch, but she didn't care because she got a kick out of hearing Angie's voice quiver whenever tittering sparrows flew through the heavy-timbered rafters, or when bats dipped and whirled in the barn's cathedral.

Out beyond the barn was an expansive pasture, edged by disheveled stonewalls, which looked as if it had once been an apple orchard, dotted with misshapen, unpruned trees. And farther yet, there was a small pond just visible from the house, with a float anchored about thirty feet from shore—a relic from a time when Beaknose had been a child visiting her grandparents. Jade pictured what it would be like to spend the entire summer swimming in the pond, but figured that Beaknose would probably keep her busy with stupid chores as well as expecting her to entertain Angie, which, in her heart of hearts, she really didn't mind doing.

Jadine sort of liked having her stepsister follow her around, hanging on her every word, even if it would have been better if she had just been a neighbor, someone who would go back to her own house when Jadine got tired of her, or when Papa came home.

Going to the new school in Rochester in the middle of the second session had been scary, and she arrived shivering, the temperature still in the 30s, her breath a faint cloud in the frigid air. Beaknose left her in the main hall and went with Angie to *her* homeroom, leaving Jadine to find her own way. It was horrible walking into the eighth grade classroom and having everyone stare at her, and, even more painful, having to eat lunch alone at an empty table in the cafeteria, all the time pretending not to care.

Neither Beaknose nor Papa asked how school was going, but eventually Jadine adjusted, admitting to herself that the kids weren't actually mean; they just totally ignored her. She felt like a fly on the wall, or better yet, she thought, a skunk, dead in the road. Well, they could be snotty all they wanted to; she really didn't care because she had her retreat, plus several acres of dense woods surrounding the farmhouse, where she could roam and forget.

To make everything worse, Beaknose constantly pulled Angie into her lap, pressing her daughter against her chest and stroking her gently, as though she were patting a kitten. Still longing for her mother even though the memory of her, by now, had grown dim, Jadine wasn't exactly jealous; it was just that *her* mother had stopped doing that probably when she was a baby and she wondered, just a little, what it would feel like now. If something happened to little Angie, maybe Beaknose would love *her*. If so, she'd consider calling her "Mama Claire" instead of Beaknose. The thought came and went so quickly that she could have pretended it never crossed her mind if she had not felt a kind of heat that fanned out in her chest, and spread up to her brain. Once, she had sipped her mother's lemonade and felt the same sensation.

Because her stepsister was afraid of the dark, Jadine had to share a bedroom with her, which was actually kind of fun, except when Papa came in to read a story or say good night. Angie always wormed her way between her and *her* Papa. Even when Jadine clung to his arm, he'd edge her aside just far enough to allow room for his *new daughter.* And Angie always got to choose which book, just as she was given the first choice in most everything because she was the youngest. *Probably because she was the prettiest, too . . . by far the prettiest.* But it was when Papa came home and ignored her that she resented Angie the most.

CHAPTER FIVE

Finally, the days became thick with the abundance of spring with drifts of wild apple blossoms floating in the air. Jadine especially loved the heavy scent of burst pine-pollen just beyond the barn. As soon as she got home from school, she wanted to be outside. One of Beaknose's rules was that Angie have an after-school snack—sliced apples and a few oatmeal cookies—but there was no place laid out on the table for Jadine.

"Can I come?" Angie begged when she caught Jadine slipping out the back door.

"Be quick. And grab a cookie for me," Jadine whispered as she strode quickly toward the woods. Angie had to run in order to keep up with her.

Wide-eyed, trusting, Angie asked her stepsister, "Where are we going?"

"You'll see."

Angie followed as Jadine clambered over boulders and crawled through tall grass, under fallen branches, used a stick to poke bugs crawling in a decaying log, and laughed when Angie asked her if they bite.

"Only if you bite first," Jadine told her.

"Where are we? We might get lost. Jadine . . ." Her small childish voice rolled on, an innocent unstoppable flood of words.

"You were the one who wanted to come," Jadine reminded her sharply. "If you want to go back, then go by yourself."

But Angie just stood there, mouth open, ribbon tangled in her hair, her legs beneath her flowered dress covered with goose bumps. Jadine gestured to a tan chipmunk scurrying away through the underbrush. "Isn't he cute?"

"Does he bite?"

Jadine did not think that question deserved an answer. "Come on. This way." She bent over to clear some low-lying branches. "Follow me."

Angie trudged along, silent for the time being, until they reached an open glade streaked with late afternoon sun. Jadine put her hand on the soft moss, a wistful expression on her face. "Feel this."

Tentatively, Angie pulled her hand from her pocket, and bent down to press her fingers into it. For a moment, she almost seemed to share her stepsister's reverence. "Like a blanket," she said.

"More comfortable than that," Jadine told her, just as, suddenly, Angie lost her footing and landed on the watery green cushion. Jadine pulled her to her feet, but not before a muddy splotch had formed on the back of her dress.

"Look what you make me do," Angie cried out. "What'll Mommy say?"

"You just tell her that you slipped," Jadine said between her teeth as she led them back through the woods. "If you say anything to get me into more trouble than I'm usually in, I will never—and I repeat, never—take you anywhere with me again."

Angie took a deep breath in an attempt to control her sobs. "Let's go home, Jadine," she said. "I promise not to tell."

"You better not," Jadine told her as she stooped to break off a clump of star-tipped moss, soft as velvet, to place in her retreat.

At school, most of the kids in her eighth-grade class had been friends since kindergarten and obviously had no intention of including Jadine in games on the playground or whatever they did after school. She knew she wasn't pretty, being taller than most of the girls, and she probably had more pimples than anyone. Not only that, but she was the only girl with short, short hair since Beaknose had insisted on keeping it that way ever since that day when Papa had chopped it off, even though it was none of her business. *None of her damn business*, Jadine often said to herself. In the bathroom, the other girls would stop speaking when she went into the toilet stall, and then laugh loudly when she started to pee. When she came out of the stall, they'd just stand there and stare at her as she washed and dried her hands. It was a small thing, but it made Jadine feel so lonely.

Angie had already made some friends who called out to her on the playground, while Jadine stood alone by the chain link fence, watching the stupid kids play that stupid game of dodge ball. For some reason, the other children just ignored her; passed around her like water around a rock. Maybe it was the clothes she wore, her boyish haircut, or just her expression. Beaknose was always telling her to get that look off her face.

As a consequence, it was a complete mystery to Jadine when that Indian kid, Billy-John Something, the boy that everyone called Bear, fell in beside her one day in April, to walk the half-mile to the farm. At thirteen, Bear was already tall and fast, with an assertive manner that made most kids defer to him—and a swift temper, which, Jadine noticed with satisfaction, even made some of them a little frightened.

They didn't talk much at first, but he sure got it— the point about rushing ahead so Angie would be left behind and would have to walk by herself.

"Where'd you get that name—Jadine?" he asked.

She felt his expectant, listening kind of silence, as if he wanted her to go on, wanted to hear her voice and whatever she chose to say. "It was my—my Mama's idea. I guess she thought it was different."

How long had it been since she'd even said the word "Mama" aloud, Jadine asked herself. Somehow, it became important to her that she make what she was feeling just now clear to him. "That mean creature I live with now is *not* my mother. My real mother ran away."

"I'm really sorry about that," Bear said. Such a simple sentence. But the way he said it made Jadine believe that he understood. She felt relief wash through her like the thawing of winter water in the spring. Someone had actually reached across the abyss that seemed to separate her from everyone else in the world.

"You're the only person I've told," she said.

Bear stopped for a moment in the middle of the road, and, picking up a stone, rolled it between the palms of his hands. "I've been thinking about you," he said. "I've decided to call you Jade because of your deep hazel-green eyes."

"Jade," she repeated, turning the name over in her mouth. *When had he noticed the color of her eyes?*

"The Chinese believe that jade stands for courage," he told her. "I think that you have courage."

"Oh no, not me—" she began.

"Bravery," he went on, undeterred. "I think you're very brave."

Was she brave? No one had ever called her that before. Then she thought of how she'd survived Mama's disappearance, a time when she thought she would die of sorrow; how she had done without any attention or care, not to mention that awful haircut; and Papa, grouchier now than ever when he came home from the print shop, demonstrating no interest in his only *real* child. And now, there was her stepmother to put up with, plus an annoying little sister she'd never wanted. And Beaknose and Papa . . . they were so wrapped up in themselves and Angie that Jadine was sure that if she just disappeared off the face of the earth, *maybe* Papa would say before going to bed, "Where's Jadine?" And Beaknose would say, "I haven't the slightest idea."

And then they would turn out the light and go to sleep.

When she thought of it like that, she supposed she *was* kind of brave.

"Thanks," she said to Bear, smiling up into his eyes. "Yes, you can call me Jade. No one else. Just you."

CHAPTER SIX

He liked to watch her in her hiding place. Dusk was closing in as Bear heard crows gather in the trees above him, gliding with amazing strength in their black bodies. He saw Jadine tilt her head toward their harsh inquisitive cries. Crouching deep in the woods that separated her farm from where he lived, he would wait, no matter how long, for her to step out of her back door, careful not to let the screen bang shut, sauntering as if she had no plan. She'd casually look around, and then dash into the woods, not far from where he was hiding, and then cut back to the shed. Sometimes her younger sister would come out and call for her, but Jade would be as still as a deer in hunting season.

Trying to put the pieces of her story together made Bear think back to the day that the Bidwells, needing help on their farm, had visited The Home for Wayward Boys that doubled as the town orphanage, and chose him, the strongest, toughest-looking kid. "We'll take that one," they had said, pointing at Billy-John.

had become his bedroom. He liked to lie on his back and watch the geometric shafts of light shine through chinks in the walls and move down the bales of hay, across the stalls and stables, while he dreamed of Jade and the freedom to be whatever he wanted to be. Now, he just hoped to Christ that Mr. Bidwell didn't drive him to do something that would wreck his plans.

Soon, he and Jadine fell into the routine of walking home together after school. Sometimes, she would hear his whistle as she approached the gigantic beech tree at the bend in the road that led to the farms where they both lived, and, following the sound, she'd find him stretched out on a long tree limb, grinning. The few times she was first to arrive at their spot, she'd wait, shifting her books impatiently from one arm to the other.

He laughed when she told him that her name for Mama Claire was "Beaknose."

"Yeah," he said. "I've got my own secret name for the man I live with. I call him Bastard Bidwell . . . BB, for short."

Now it was Jadine's turn to laugh. Except she was no longer Jadine. With Bear, she was someone new. Jade. A pretty girl with green eyes and a spring to her step who had someone who listened to her and appreciated her for who she was. She wanted to know more about Bear.

"What'd BB do to deserve that name?"

"Here. Look." Bear stopped, and pulled up his pant leg to his knee. There was an angry-looking scar about three inches long on the front of his leg.

"It still aches. BB hit me twice with the shovel because I'd stayed at school to research a paper. So I'd been a little late. The shit that is supposed to be shoveled every day wasn't going anywhere."

"My God, that looks awful."

"It's a deep cut, all right," he agreed, "but actually it didn't bleed much. I didn't make a sound, not a whimper. I wouldn't give the bastard that satisfaction. He could beat me to death and I wouldn't cry out," he added proudly.

"Didn't they take you to a hospital?" she asked.

"Are you kidding? As if they'd give a damn. I just pulled the gash together with masking tape. All BB's wife did was warn me not to use up the whole roll."

"And you call *me* brave," Jadine said, as they set off together again. "We're peas in a pod."

That was the day Bear told her where he got the name Billy-John.

"You could've froze to death!" she exclaimed. "Those drunks saved your life."

"I guess." He shrugged, as if it didn't matter much. "More than anything, I wish I had that jacket with *Kuruk* printed on it. Something that belonged to my real family. That would really be something."

Jade thought of Mama. Compared to Bear, she was lucky because she had memories of Mama, good ones, and bits and pieces of Mama's clothes and belongings. But Bear seemed a lot less upset about being abandoned than she did, telling about things so matter-of-factly, as if he'd been saying he was born on a Tuesday, under a full moon. She wished she could just accept that Mama had had her own good reasons for leaving and for staying away, and whatever they were, it had nothing to do with her—Jadine. That was just the way life was. Bear could teach her how to reason like that, she thought.

When she got home, Angie tattled. "Jadine's got a boyfriend."

Beaknose turned from the sink and looked Jadine up and down in a way that made her feel naked and embarrassed.

"Who is it?" she demanded.

And when Jadine didn't answer, Angie said, "It's that Indian boy who lives with the Bidwells."

"That foster kid?" Beaknose frowned. "You better pay attention, Jadine Tomecelli. Bonnie Bidwell told me he's sullen and ungrateful. And after all they've done, taking him from the orphanage and all. You watch yourself, girl, because I'm *not* taking care of any little babies around here."

"It's not like that," Jadine told her, adding under her breath, "not that you would ever understand."

CHAPTER SEVEN

Summer finally came. Of course Papa hadn't made it to her eighth grade graduation. Not that she had received any prizes for anything, but Jadine felt loneliness creep under her skin when she heard clapping and loud whistles for what seemed like every name except hers. Beaknose came at the end of the ceremony, not to see her graduate, but to pick up Angie.

The summer days on the farm seemed long to Jadine with Angie constantly on her heels, making it even more of a challenge now to get to the retreat without being noticed. Both girls were expected to work in the kitchen garden, first thing every morning, weeding between the plants and picking beetles off the leaves. Jadine had to admit that she was pleased that Angie had to help, too. Fair was fair.

Even at night, she couldn't escape Beaknose's influence. The room that once had been her stepmother's as a child, now made smaller by a pair of single beds and two bureaus placed there for Jadine and Angie to share, was reminiscent of a different era with its tiny pink-flowered wallpaper and water stains near the ceiling on one wall. There was an old orange and brown braided rug that Beaknose's grandmother had made from discarded work clothes. At least that's what Beaknose had told Jadine, warning her sternly to keep her magic markers away from it.

Jadine came to realize that her only privacy, one that could not be violated, was when she slept. Except that was when Mama invaded her dreams. When she was still half-asleep, she could almost believe that her mother's spirit was really with her because how could she fabricate a presence with such convincing evidence by simple longing? But then, awakening, confused and agitated, Jadine felt she had been tricked and abandoned. Always abandoned.

Although the girls were supposed to be helping in the kitchen, one glorious Saturday morning, Beaknose gave in to their pleas to cool off in the pond. Angie was a good swimmer for an almost ten-year-old, and besides, they were somewhat visible from the summer kitchen at the back of the house where Beaknose did all of her canning.

As the two girls lay stretched out on the old sun-heated float which rocked gently on water ruffled by a soft breeze, Jadine thought about starting high school. What would it be like, she wondered, to be popular? She was tall for her age, and her body was filling out. In the bright sun, her hair, which Beaknose had finally let her grow until it touched her shoulders, shone like polished chestnuts. Lying flat on her stomach, she looked down through the still water at weeds rocking subtly in the invisible spring-fed currents beneath the surface. Water bugs zipped across the surface, leaving rippling silver trails.

She and Angie had been playing that forbidden game in which one of them would jump off the float, swim out way over their head, and then yell "Help! Help! I'm drowning," at which point, the other would "rescue" them.

"Let's play it again," Angie had begged. "Please, please, Jadine."

"I will, if you hide in the attic when Papa comes home tonight. And you have to stay there until I say you can come out."

"But I don't like it in the attic, it's scary up there," Angie whined in the same way she always did when she wanted Papa to pay attention to her. "It's like the barn."

Jadine turned over and closed her eyes, letting the afternoon sun beat down on her while she waited for Angie to give in.

What would it be like to run away? She had watched Beaknose stuff Papa's pay envelope in her pocket, and then throw her fat arms around his neck. It would be easy enough to steal some money from her purse and sneak out after they went to bed. She would hitchhike straight to Canada—if she could only remember the return address on Mama's letters, and when she found her, ask her why she left. Jadine was beginning to think it was Papa's fault. But it was Mama's fault, too. She could have taken Jadine with her. And so, no matter what excuses Mama might come up with, Jadine would turn her back and . . .

"Okay, I will." Angie had appeared suddenly, holding on to the edge of the float.

"Will what?"

"Hide in the attic."

"Promise?"

"Yeah," Angie said in a small voice.

Jadine sat up, ready to begin the game, when she thought she spotted something moving among the high-bush blueberries along the east side of the pond. The sun reflecting off the water's surface made it difficult to see clearly.

Was it Bear, she wondered, ready to plunge into the water and join their game?

Angie pushed away from the float and swam far out, treading water way over her head. "I'm ready," she called.

Jadine stood, gave an exaggerated stretch. "Okay," she shouted back, her voice skimming over the water.

"Help, help, I'm drowning," Angie yelled, laughing and splashing, flailing her arms in mock panic, waiting for her stepsister to swim out and grab her under her chin.

Maybe because Bear *might* be watching, Jadine, holding her nose, did an elaborate cannonball off the float, banging her leg hard on the edge as she went in. It hurt like heck, and when she surfaced, she yelled out to Angie, "I'm not playing anymore. I hurt my leg." Then, taking a deep breath, she let herself glide downward into the spring-fed depths, doing the breaststroke under water until her heart felt like it was going to burst.

Emerging from the water onto the sandy spit of beach that jutted out into the pond, Jadine sat down stiffly and started to rub her leg when she noticed that the pond had become still.

Where the heck was Angie? Jumping to her feet, she scanned the water beyond the float. And saw nothing. As a slow awareness began to grip her, she threw herself into the pond, swimming as fast as she could, her arms working like pistons.

When she came up for air, her screams for Angie pierced the silence and hurled themselves across the meadow and into the kitchen where Mama Claire was canning bread 'n butter pickles.

CHAPTER EIGHT

Yelling for help, Jadine raced toward the house. After screeching into the phone, begging for someone to come, Jadine watched her stepmother through the open doorway, running toward the pond, calling Angie's name. If only she could clearly reconstruct what had happened, Jadine thought, she could then unbraid the strands of fear from the strands of anger inside her. She kept seeing the afternoon's events break down moment by moment. The pain she had felt across her chest when she swam out looking for Angie had been nothing compared to how she imagined Angie must have felt to sink down deep and breathe water into her lungs.

Never, for as long as she lived, would she forget the look on Papa's face when suddenly, upon hearing about Angie, his eyes had bulged and he slid from his chair, his cheeks flaming red, then turning as gray as clay.

Beaknose, who had been escorted back to the house by a policewoman after they had retrieved Angie's body, just stared at Papa while he struggled to breathe. Slowly, deliberately, she had stepped over him on her way to

the bathroom, and refused to come out even when the
EMTs arrived and took Papa to the hospital. The lock
on that bathroom door had cried out an accusation.

Jadine's trembling presence in the hallway went
unnoticed, where no one had even stopped to speak
to her or offer comfort. She sat on those wide antique
boards with her back against the bathroom door, playing
the scene at the pond over and over again. *Angie's a
strong swimmer . . . what could've happened?* She would give
anything in the world to turn the clock back, to play
the drowning game with Angie, swim out as she had so
many times before, to bring her safely to shore. If only,
if only . . . And she would never have made Angie stay in
the attic. She had just been teasing her about that.

In those bleak lonely hours, during the longest day
of her life, Jadine knew that this was an ending—a part
of her life to which there would be no return. In a way,
it was even worse than Mama leaving. Angie had been
the younger one; Jadine was supposed to have been
responsible. Two splinters deep in the pad of Jadine's
finger were a stark reminder of the moment when,
clinging to the float, she realized that Angie was gone.
She hoped they would stay there forever, so she would
never forget how Angie died.

Later that night, the police returned and smashed
their way into the bathroom, where Beaknose lay
sprawled on the floor, her face twisted, a grotesque
grimace carved into her features.

✼ ✼ ✼

Papa took a stroke from the shock of it all, and
Mama Claire just curled up and died. That's what all
the neighbors said about them after the accident. Some

thought that although Angie's mother might have died of a sleeping pill overdose, the true reason for her death was that her heart was broken—on that, they all agreed.

Jadine cried inconsolably, and Papa never got over losing another wife. Instead, he withered away until there was nobody left for Jadine to love. And certainly, nobody loved her.

Except for Bear.

But she did not know that until later.

CHAPTER NINE

The Rochester Church ladies, banding together to do the right thing, took it upon themselves to make arrangements for Papa after conferring with the New Hampshire Department of Children, Youth and Families as to who would be responsible for Jadine Tomecelli who was about to enter high school. Someone—Jadine never knew the details—had sold the farm property and paid the proceeds to the nursing home where Papa had gone directly after two weeks in the hospital. The caseworker at the DCYF was only too happy to grant the women from the church guardianship, relieved to be able to remove a file from the very tall stack on his desk, each one of which contained a sad story, since there were never enough families willing to take in children who had been forgotten, lost, and mistreated.

"It seems like a good solution," he had commented. "I hope Jadine knows how lucky she is."

Since Jadine was not old enough to be a decision-maker about her life, her new "Aunties" agreed to pass their charge around from house to house, each one keeping her for six months at a time, until she finished high school. She became what the church called their Mercy Project.

Amid all the confusion, Jadine heard someone say: ". . . the Bible tells us that to be righteous, one must look after widows and orphans. . ." She could hardly imagine what her future held, but somehow, she was hopeful.

✧ ✧ ✧

Raymond Tomecelli did not recognize his daughter when, at last, weeks after Angie's death, she visited him at the nursing home. The day was clear with the sharp penetrating bite in the air that can come in mid-October. Jadine had walked the half-mile, head down, scuffing through leaves—the sunlight, pale and thin, already fading. Standing for a moment in the doorway of the room that Papa shared with five other men, it struck her how quiet they were. No one was talking to anyone else. Instead, all she heard was snoring and moaning and gibberish which bounced against the yellowed stucco walls and trickled down onto the vinyl floor, where a dizzying pattern of large beige circles swirled on a worn brown background. Overhead, Patsy Cline lamented, almost cheerfully, about Heartaches, with a capital 'H', as if it was something that these men, even in their diminished states, didn't know about. Jadine wanted to rip down the blinds that were lowered against the sun, shred them, scream at the top of her lungs. Something. Anything.

Shivering, Jadine pulled her sweater closed across her chest as she entered the room. Her heart pounded the same irregular beat as the day that Angie died— when Papa had lain gasping for air on the kitchen floor, right after Beaknose had accused Jadine of killing her daughter. "*She* did it," Beaknose had screamed at Papa, sweeping her arm toward Jadine. "She's an evil girl. Evil. Evil."

Shaking off the memory of that nightmare, pressing it back into the depth of her consciousness, Jadine crossed the room and knelt, accosted by the smell of urine, next to her father's chair where he sat, strapped in.

"It's Jadine, Papa," she said, reaching to touch his trembling hand, so white, except for the traces of printer's ink sunk indelibly in the deep lines of his fingers, her long chestnut hair brushing his arm. He winced at the sight of it—or was it the sound of her voice?—shaking his head in slow motion, back and forth in denial. A soft animal-like keening erupted from his loose lips; drool ran down a deep furrow in his chin to the left of his mouth. Jade watched it drip slowly onto his lap. She thought maybe he was trying to say, "No." Or was it "go"? She was suddenly intensely aware of just how much her father's weakness had cost her, and, overcome with shame and anger, knew that the last possible shred of normalcy in her life had slipped away forever.

She bit her thumbnail until it bled.

This was not my fault. He . . . He turned me into an orphan.

He never loved me anyway, she told herself, vowing that she would not visit him again.

CHAPTER TEN

Initially, the Rochester "Aunties" had taken on her pain, molded it for her, expecting her to be grateful in return. But Jadine noticed that whenever the time came for her to leave, they'd send her off with it still intact. She came to think of each move as an *assignment*, during which she had to meet the six-month requirements before packing her belongings, and, with her retreat box securely under her arm, waited at the end of the driveway to be picked up by the next "Auntie." It made her squirm with shame to remember the hope she'd had in the beginning, when they had treated her in a rush of kindness and curiosity, like a stray dog.

Having to dress in hand-me-downs or clothes from that musty Silver Lining second-hand shop on Webster Street, Jadine grew to hate wearing other people's stuff, stinking as it did of sweat or stale perfume. By junior year, she started shoplifting at the Wal-Mart in Farmington. She could feel her bowels in an uproar each time she stole something, the fear of being caught overshadowed by wanting so badly to dress like the other girls in her class. Not that it made them any friendlier, the stuck-up creeps.

The "Aunties" did not suspect her occasional thefts because she wasn't in one home long enough for them to notice. Jadine knew one thing for sure; she was a burden to them all, a cross to bear, a project that would garner praise for their phony do-gooder ways long after she was gone. *The Bitches of Rochester would always feel good about themselves.* Jadine hated being beholden to anyone and was determined that once she graduated from high school, she would never again allow herself to be in the position of having to do anything against her will. But, for now, she would bide her time and hold her tongue, even if it killed her.

Over the next four years, Jadine lived in a cocoon of indifference. Nothing seemed to provide her with the comfort of feeling that she belonged. During these years of expected shifting alliances, she learned to keep her feelings to herself. While *she* cleaned the "Aunties'" houses, *their* kids were playing school sports or taking part in a host of extracurricular activities. She babysat their younger kids and did the laundry, since everyone made it clear that she should show her gratitude by making herself useful. Otherwise, she existed like an annoying shadow among these charitable families.

Her only pleasure was Bear, who had become a constant companion. Whenever they could slip away, they roamed the woods together, stopping to sit on boulders, or to stretch out on a bed of pine needles, staring up through the branches. Sometimes Bear would break the comfortable silence by offering her bits and pieces of himself.

"After the DCYF delivered me into foster care," he told her, "my foster mother used the support money from the state to play the slot machines at Foxwoods down in Rhode Island. She was obsessed with gambling. I remember spending hours on end in Foxwoods' daycare program. I always dreaded the trips back to New Hampshire because then she was meaner than ever."

Bear leaned up on his elbow and stared intently at Jadine. "She'd sit crouched over the steering wheel saying over and over how pissed she was, and that if they didn't close the friggin' daycare so damn early, she could have won back her losses. And she blamed me, too. Just for existing, I guess. She'd give hard nuggies on my head or a twisting pinch on my arm if I made a sound in the back seat. God, how I hated her."

Tears welled in Jadine's eyes. At least when she had been that little, Mama had still been there.

"Don't feel sorry for me," Bear told her. "I just want you to understand how it was with me. I used to shit my pants and stuff them behind a radiator or in the back of her closet. I kept doing it until she gave up when I was four and sent me to The Home. She apparently told them I was incorrigible. At least that was the word they used."

Bear laughed heartily, and flopped down on his back. Breaking off a pine bough, he held it first to his nose and then to hers.

"Did you hate The Home as much as I hate my *assignments*?"

"No. I was glad to live where I could be anyone I wanted to be. There was something almost welcoming about it. All I had to do was follow the rules. And . . ." Bear paused, put his hand on her cheek, turning her face to his. "And I quit shitting my pants overnight."

"You *are* incorrigible, Bear," Jadine told him, grinning. "Now tell me why you call yourself an Indian, when the teachers refer to you as Native American?"

"I like being different," he said, shrugging. "I'm glad I'm not like the other kids at The Home—those dumb jerks had no idea who they were or where they came from, and didn't care, either."

Jade remembered how pitifully she had mourned her mother, and found his intensity almost intimidating. She didn't need to tell him about that part of her history.

"I found out that I'm from the Pawnee tribe," he told her, "and that Kuruk means Bear."

"I guess that's why you love the woods . . . it must be in your blood."

"How about *your* blood? What makes you love the woods so?" Bear gave her the smile that always pierced her heart.

"It started out as an escape, but now . . . there's you," she said, reaching out for him. The kiss that followed seemed to last forever, and afterwards, as they lay face to face among pinecones, acorns, and last year's leaves softened by spring's thaw, he sculpted his body to hers, and with his large calloused hands, touched as gently as if he had found something small and fragile that he didn't want to break. The tension she felt, the coiling inside her, was exquisite. Unbuttoning his shirt, Jadine placed her face on his smooth, muscular chest.

Having Bear in her life was comforting in a way that she didn't even try to understand. All she knew was that Bear provided an undeniable protective shield, a bond that followed her from *assignment* to *assignment*. They were no longer orphans. They had each other. And when she was with him, she dared to believe in a future.

CHAPTER ELEVEN

Although Jadine was built like an athlete and unusually well-coordinated, she hated organized sports. She was always the last person chosen for sides; no one ever hit, threw, or kicked the ball to her, and if her team won, she was never part of the celebration that followed.

Beginning sophomore year, the Gladstones were her third *assignment*, one which was particularly distasteful because Melvin and Cynthia's charming daughter, Rebecca, spent her free time at school either ignoring or ridiculing Jadine.

In a burst of some peculiar sort of altruism, "Auntie Cindy" insisted that Jadine join the soccer team. "It's such a wholesome activity," she said, "and a chance to make new friends," leaving Jadine to wonder what kind of planet she was from.

On Fridays, girls' soccer shared the field with football practice. One bright October afternoon, when, in the distance, maples burned like flames in the crisp air, Jadine was playing hard, as always, when, out of the blue, Rebecca, who was her team captain, shoved her roughly from behind, throwing her forward onto her knees. Thinking it was someone from the opposing team, Jadine twisted on the ground to see her number. She was surprised to see that it was Rebecca, but then remembered having heard her complain bitterly to her parents about Jadine's *assignment* at their house.

"Just because you want to do charity work, Mom," Rebecca had said, knowing that Jadine was within easy hearing distance, "doesn't mean I want to. It's so embarrassing to have her living in our house."

It was an effort just trying to breathe, but no one seemed to notice—not her teammates or the stinking coach, even though she stayed on her knees, gasping for air. Telling herself that she should concentrate on counting the days, Jadine was just attempting to stand when she heard a familiar bird whistle and saw Bear watching her from the adjacent field, suited up for football, bigger and taller than the other players. And that was all she needed. Head held high, she rejoined the team.

✼ ✼ ✼

"Are you okay?" Bear asked later on the way home after practice.

"Yeah," she said, watching the last gray light of the afternoon settle over the field. "Just forget it."

"Hard to." He suddenly stopped walking, and pulled her against his chest. She loved how tightly he squeezed her, how strong he was. For a long moment, their bodies were pressed together. He smelled of sweat and something else, something intensely male. His hands lightly traced the muscles of her back and shoulders until she drew away from him.

"She hates me, Bear," she told him. "That's all. People don't change."

What Jadine didn't know how to put into words, even to Bear, was her fear that no matter where she went, she'd always be the pariah she was now. All she could think about was the end of high school and being able to leave with Bear. When that happened, everything would be all right. She was certain of it.

Two days later, the buzz at school was all about Rebecca.

"Someone pushed Rebecca on the stairs," they said. "She chipped a front tooth and broke her wrist."

"Who did it?"

"Nobody saw it happen."

"Was it an accident?"

"Who knows? She might have missed a step."

"There goes her soccer for the year."

CHAPTER TWELVE

Jadine's July-to-December *assignment* during her senior year was the only one in which the family treated her half-decently. Albert and Merle LaPierre had just one child, eight-month-old Samantha, who was as cute as a button and seemed to favor Jadine, something that touched her in an unfamiliar way, an emotion that she dared not trust. It was a response on her part that was reinforced by the fact that "Auntie Merle" would never leave the baby alone with her, not because she thought Jadine was unreliable, but as Samantha's mother, she explained, she was too attached to leave her with a babysitter. *Not ever.*

Half-decent treatment in this family only meant that they were not outright cruel. But they made no effort to hide the fact that taking her in was an obligation, particularly given the gossip about her that had been passed on from other households. Everyone, it seemed, had made a judgment about Jadine Tomecelli.

Wouldn't she like to write a report on each family, and have it count for something—post it in the *Foster's Daily*, or on the Rochester city hall bulletin board?

Damn Mama and Papa to hell forever.

Because the only thing that was required of her by the LaPierres was household chores, the *assignment* with them seemed longer than most, and Jadine spent some of each vacation day in the Rochester library. She had taken the list of summer reading handed out by the English teacher seriously, and surprisingly, so had Bear, so it was only natural that they should have fallen into a routine of meeting there. Holding hands when they walked home from the library, Jadine felt a heartbreaking surge of self-pity in the most childish and brutal way when Bear asked about her past. Something, not of her doing, cast a shadow so enormous that, when they were apart, it covered her and everything around her. She was amazed to find out that, instead of sharing her bitterness, Bear had been able to put his past behind him. When he pointed out that they had both grown up without love from any parent, for some reason he wasn't angry about it the way she was. She envied his ability to let go of things.

Meanwhile, when the word got around school that they were a "couple," attitudes changed. No one nominated her for homecoming queen, but at least she no longer felt like an outcast or dreaded going to school. When they were together, she felt insulated from harm. She supposed that if Bear hadn't been tall, assertive, *and* the quarterback on the football team, and if she hadn't been the only girl he'd ever paid attention to, she wouldn't have been accepted. She loved it when girls flirted with Bear. He would look right through them, totally focused on Jadine. Yes, she enjoyed that, every time it happened.

That fall, Jadine spent her free time hiking through the conservation land that backed up to the

LaPierre's property, always listening for Bear's whistle, looking forward to his sudden appearances, loving his company.

✫ ✫ ✫

On the last day in December, she wandered in the wintry woods, hoping to meet Bear, raising her face to the falling snow so light and delicate that it felt like powder against her eyelids. Pine trees, laden with ice, creaked in the silence until, suddenly, she heard voices coming from the abandoned sandpit that bordered an old logging road.

Peering through the brush, Jadine spied four boys she had seen at school, standing around a small campfire, stamping their feet against the cold and guzzling beer. Laughing raucously, they were crunching cans against their foreheads and then tossing them into a pile. When one of the boys unzipped his pants and proceeded to pee into the fire, Jadine turned to retrace her steps and found herself face-to-face with Ted Jenkins, one of Bear's teammates.

"Hey, Jay-deeeen. Gettin' your jollies watching us waggin' our weenies?" he demanded with a lopsided grin. A six-pack of beer was dangling from his left hand. "Wanna see my dick? Wanna hold it?"

"You're a bunch of pigs," she said, shoving him away from her as he fumbled with his zipper. "You better back off."

"Who's a pig?" Dropping the beer in the snow, he grabbed her arm. "Football's over. We don't have to kow-tow to your boyfriend from The Home anymore. I would've been the quarterback if it hadn't been for that damn Injun." Holding her roughly, he called to his buddies. "Look who likes to watch us piss. *Miss Jay-deeeen Nobody.*"

His voice ricocheted through the bare branches of the birches and settled closely among the boughs of the prickly junipers.

As his friends approached, Jadine struggled frantically to free her arm when, without warning, Ted hooked his foot behind her legs, and pushed her backwards so roughly that she landed against the frozen, snow-covered ground with a thump that momentarily knocked the wind out of her. Lying on her back, she kicked frantically, attempting to keep the gang of boys at bay as they surrounded her.

"She likes to watch us takin' a leak," Ted told the others, so they all unzipped their flies and began to urinate on her. Jadine screamed in a wild, screeching voice when she felt the hot, acid liquid splash her face.

A roaring sound reached through her terror and then a *thwack* resounded through the forest when Jadine saw the trunk of a pine tree hurled straight at Ted, felling him like a bowling pin.

"Jesus, Bear, what the fuck?" one of the boys yelled.

"You're going to pay for this," Bear said, and even though it was directed at the boys, Jadine felt their fear. Scrambling to her feet, she scooped up a handful of snow, scrubbing her face raw with it. When she saw Bear reach down for an icy lichen-covered stone by his boot, she grabbed his hand, pulling him away. The look on his face was frightening.

"No more. *Please, Bear,*" she cried as, with one quick motion, he scooped her up, cradled her to his chest, and strode away through the darkening forest.

CHAPTER THIRTEEN

The next day was January first, transition day. The LaPierres had driven Jadine across town to her last *assignment,* probably only too glad to be done with their obligation, she thought, as well as congratulating themselves that precious Samantha was unharmed because they had never allowed Jadine to babysit. Not for one minute did either LaPierre ask *her* what had really happened in the woods or if she was all right. *And why? Because, it wouldn't have made a difference to them.*

Standing in the hallway of the O'Days modest ranch house with her backpack, the retreat box, and one large, handled shopping bag, Jadine waited while her new and final *assignment* "parents" argued in the kitchen.

I can do this final mile, she told herself. Nothing lasts forever.

"I don't want her. It's as simple as that," Jadine heard Stephanie telling her husband. "She's a trouble maker. That's what everyone is saying."

"You committed to it over three years ago," Ed O'Day reminded her. "The whole town did. It's our turn. Christ, Stephie, it's only for six months. Have a heart. We'll establish some strict rules and keep her busy. June'll be here before you know it."

The front door was still open, and Jadine stared at Mr. O'Day's squad car in the driveway. Somehow, the thought of living in a cop's house freaked her out.

Believe me, "Auntie Stephie," I don't want to be here any more than you want me.

Acquiescing, Mrs. O'Day set the rules: Jadine was to go to the library right after school to do her homework. Furthermore, she was not to leave there until five, at which time she was to come directly home, help with dinner and cleanup, then go to her room where she was allowed to listen to the radio, as long as it was set low enough so that it couldn't be heard in the rest of the house. Weekends, she was expected to make herself useful around the place. Absolutely no dating. And no bringing friends home.

No wonder their only child, a fifteen-year-old daughter, had run away.

Jadine made up her mind to stick it out by following the rules. But she would not talk, just reply in monosyllables—be nothing but a deaf and dumb blob whose only ambition was to exist until June.

January second, the day everyone returned to school, Bear sat stiffly in Mr. Matthews' office where he waited forty-five minutes for the principal to talk to him. Waited and simmered. This is not unlike the way he had been treated when he had been in trouble at The Home. But this time, he told himself, he was in the right even if Ted *was* in the hospital with a concussion, and he knew it. Meanwhile, he could see Ted's parents through the glass of the office door, his father shaking his fist at the principal. Mr. and Mrs. Jenkins hadn't even looked at Bear when they had stormed by him earlier. But now, he figured, they wanted someone to punish him big time.

Bear was thinking about the past four years during which he had watched over Jade as though he had been born to protect her, just as he would have a sister or mother. The idea of him protecting a mother he didn't even know made him smile. And the thought of receiving protection *from* a mother was a joke. It had never happened. Not from the moment of his birth. Truth be known, he didn't give a damn about his mother, but with Jade, it was different. Something churned in his chest when he whispered her name.

Other than Jade, what Bear cared about most were the animals on the Bidwell farm. The cows had to be milked every morning before school and again at the end of the day, as BB never tired of reminding him. They grazed on twenty acres of pastureland, fenced off from the cultivated fields by barbed wire. Going to fetch the cows was a favorite task. It was satisfying to follow their deeply rutted path, where there were no manmade sounds or smells on the way to the tender cool grasses of the pasture, the natural fragrance of which was almost overwhelming in summer. On balance, he hated, however, working the fields, mostly because BB was on his case every minute, always feeling free to use his fist or his boot to make a point. Bear was stupid, or too slow, he liked to say. Rather than trying to please the bastard, Bear wanted to tell him to fuck off, right to his face. But instead, he concentrated on staying focused on graduating and leaving Rochester forever, with Jade— his plan since he'd first laid eyes on her.

And now, the middle of our senior year—we're almost there. What have I gotten us into? Is Matthews going to back me up— do the right thing??

The principal waved him into his office and started speaking before Bear had dropped onto the straight-backed wooden chair in front of his oversized oak desk, launching his attack immediately.

"What the hell did you think you were doing, clubbing Ted so badly that he had to be hospitalized? A teammate? A kid who might have been quarterback if I hadn't pushed for you?"

"I *was* quarterback, Mr. Matthews, because I was the better player, and not because you pulled strings for me," Bear said, making a show of staring at the trophy the principal had won when he had attended Rochester High years before. "You wanted a win for your school and I got it for you."

"That's beside the point, young man," Mr. Matthews replied, slightly flustered. "You should be glad that Ted's parents haven't had you up on a charge of assault and battery. There's no doubt in my mind that you need to learn a lesson you'll never forget."

"What about Ted and the others? Are they going to be disciplined?" Bear suspected that he was moving toward a consequence to his anger so ugly that he could almost feel the shape of it, and yet he could not think of a way to keep it from happening.

A curtain that seemed to drop behind the principal's eyes was all too familiar, and Bear knew as surely as the sun would rise, that, whatever it was, the man's mind was set in stone.

Just then, Miss O'Donnell, the science teacher, opened the principal's door without knocking. "I just heard what happened to Jadine," she exclaimed. "What are you going to do about it? Because it's an outrage."

The principal's only response was to slam the door in her face.

His words erupted suddenly. "It's jail time or the army," he told Bear. "As of right now, you're officially kicked out of Rochester High. No suspension, no coming back. And no graduation."

"Kicked out? Without you even hearing my side of the story?" Bear could feel his face settling into a hard mask. "Did they tell you what Ted and the others did?" he demanded defiantly. "*I saw them, Mr. Matthews.* Are you going to let them get away with having assaulted Jadine, taking a *piss* on her, as well as drinking under age?"

Bear rose to his feet, both hands fisted.

"You sit your ass right back in that chair," the principal told him. "That's for me to handle. I know all I need to know."

"The hell you do."

"Don't get fresh with me if you know what's good for you."

"Good for me? They attacked Jadine and look a leak on her face—*on her face.* Would it be okay if they did that to your daughter?"

A cold light fell through the window, bringing with it a vision of Jade, lying on the ground. Rage surged through Bear's veins.

"That's just about enough," the principal said. "Now shut your mouth and calm down. The truth is, you kids from The Home are hopeless. I gave you an opportunity to make something of yourself, Billy-John, and what do you do? Send the son of a School Board member to the hospital over some dubious complaint from a girl whose word can hardly be trusted. What were you thinking, boy?"

"What was *I* thinking, you bastard?" Bear shouted. "What are *you* thinking? How about some justice? How about kicking *them* out? Are you really just going to pimp for Ted's father and the rest of them? I actually thought you might be fair, but you've chosen the wrong side of the playing field this time." Bear had the feeling of being an observer, watching a tragedy being acted out without the power to interfere. He leaned forward and with one sweep of his arm, everything on the principal's desk flew to the floor.

In an instant, the principal was on the phone calling for security. "I need a student escorted out of my office and off school grounds, immediately," he said, holding the phone out defensively. "Now, what'll it be, Billy-John?" he said as he picked up the enlistment paper and a pen from the floor and slapped them on his desk. "Jail or the army? Because, although Ted's family may not bring charges, I will."

"You can't make me. You don't have the power to do that."

"Just try me, boy. You don't have a clue as to what I can do. Make a choice. You've got one minute to decide."

"You're not going to break me, *Mr. Matthews*," Bear said. "Nobody's going to." With that, he grabbed the pen, signed the paper, and stomped out of the office as he heard the principal shouting to be on the eleven o'clock bus to Manchester.

Thinking about leaving Jadine, he experienced something sudden and unfamiliar, a tightness in his throat and water in his eyes.

CHAPTER FOURTEEN

In the Rochester High School records, Jadine Tomecelli's personality profile stated that she was an immature adolescent, battling conflicts resulting from a number of early traumas, including so many losses ranging from abandonment by her mother, the drowning of her stepsister, to the death of her stepmother and the estrangement her father. Furthermore, it stated, she was resentful of adult authority and preoccupied with the fear of being abandoned. "She suffers from a deep sense of rejection," the report concluded, "and resents the great sacrifices and kindness offered to her by the townspeople of Rochester."

During Bear's interview with the principal, Jadine had been told to wait down the hall in the secretary's office. She had had no trouble locating her folder under the "T" file, and quickly, without looking at it, shoved it into her backpack just as the principal appeared in the doorway, and told her to follow him to his office.

The surface of his desk looked like he had dumped all the drawers onto it; his face was pasty white, and his shirt was stained under his arms.

"You are on probation, young lady, for your part in the incident," he barked at Jadine just as the door closed behind her.

Incident—is that what you call it?

"One little insolent comment, one show of defiance, one negative report from your foster care parents, and you're out," he told her, glowering from behind his littered desk.

She said nothing. It was, as far as she could see, her only recourse. Obviously he didn't give a crap about what had happened to her. *It was off his radar, the bastard.* He stared at her a minute more, probably waiting for a response. But, over the years, she had become the master of angry silence.

"Answer me, dammit," he demanded. "Do you understand me or not?"

"Yes, I understand," she told him, meeting his eyes defiantly. *Believe me, Mr. Matthews, I understand a good deal better than you think.*

As Jadine trudged to the library after school, wondering what had happened to Bear, she heard his whistle from a path behind her. Relieved, she ran to greet him. Not caring whether anyone saw them, almost roughly, he crushed her to his chest, burying his face in her hair. Jadine wound her arms around his neck, felt his heart pounding wildly against hers.

"What happened?" she asked. Pulling back to look at him, she saw that in spite of his usual iron control, he seemed to have aged ten years in as many hours.

"The bastard kicked me out of school," he told her. "He had the papers needed for me to enlist in the army right there on his desk and he—he gave me a choice between signing them and being charged with assault." Bear wasn't wearing a jacket, light snow glistened in his black hair.

"And the bus leaves in twenty minutes."

She stared at him, appalled, as every hope that she had ever had for happiness faded and died. "They won't even let you graduate?" she cried.

"No, they want me gone. But I had to see you, Jade." Her name staggered out on an uneven breath and he pressed his mouth against hers with such passion, she moaned, and her knees buckled.

"I'll write to you at the O'Days," he told her. "Stay strong, my Jade, only one more *assignment*. I will love you forever."

With that, he turned away, snow crunching under his footsteps, leaving her stripped of all her dreams.

Jadine stood perfectly still. The freezing air seemed to punch tiny holes in her skin. She reached back to flip her hood over her head. Somehow Bear had been blamed and now his dream of graduating was over, and she was alone—again. She became aware of a sensation like vertigo, a sound in her head like the whipping wind.

"I love you, too, Bear," she called out over and over again, long after he was out of sight.

CHAPTER FIFTEEN

The sign on the library door read "Closed Due to Storm". Without so much as a glimpse of the sun, January had passed, and now, near the end of February, not even four o'clock, storm clouds had closed over Rochester like a lid shutting on a coffin. Looking at the snow falling, tiny floating ghosts spinning in and out of the blue-black beyond, Jadine knew that even though "Auntie Stephie" would be bullshit, she had no choice but to go home early.

The worst part of the O'Day *assignment* was the constant smell of bleach coming not only from the laundry room, but the kitchen, the two bathrooms, and the mudroom, always making her eyes smart. It was there the minute she entered the house. And then, she heard laughter coming from the O'Day's bedroom. Had Ed come home early? Checking the driveway, she did not see his cruiser.

Uh oh, sneaky "Auntie Stephie," do you think a sterile house implies a sterile life? Huh, "Auntie Stephie"? You're busted, she thought. Is this why she told me not to ever come back to the house right after school? One plus one equals an affair that must have been going on for a long time, and upstanding Officer O'Day would be the last to know.

Wiping up the slush she had tracked in, Jadine retraced her steps to the car she had seen by the side of the road, half-buried now in snow, and, with numb fingers, wrote the license plate number inside the cover of her biology book before retreating to the garage and waiting, shivering, not only from the cold, but with the excitement of her discovery.

Although her guidance counselor had said Jadine had considerable potential, she barely earned her degree thanks to her depression and isolation since Bear left. Nonetheless, graduation day finally arrived. Waiting for her name to be called, sitting in the intense June sun, Jadine muttered under her breath that she couldn't give a damn who was there that day or why. All of her *assignment* parents attended her graduation, though, beaming and clapping as though they had something to do with who she'd turned out to be. Well, actually, she knew that they had all had a lot to do with molding her into an introverted, angry person. But all she really cared about now was that, along with her diploma, came her walking papers.

Screw you, Rochester. Screw you, "Aunties." May you have the lives you deserve.

Her one monumental regret was Bear, who had not written, not even once, although "Auntie Stephie" might have intercepted his letters—the bitch'd had plenty of time to throw them out before she was allowed to go home, or, was Bear blaming her for his getting kicked out without graduating? His silence had so lacerated her heart that she had forced herself to dismiss the memory of him. And his declaration of love.

He'll be all right because he's a survivor, she assured herself, and besides, it was his decision—she hadn't asked him to hit that asshole with that stump.

It was so unfair. None of those rotten perverts had ever been punished for what they had done to her.

Only Bear.

In addition to the money she acquired from pant pockets and wallets lying carelessly around her various "homes," she now had the money they had donated, fifty dollars per family, as a final gesture of their good intentions, before putting her on a bus for Boston. Was it, she wondered, their way of apologizing? Or did it signal a final dismissal? In any case, she was glad to have it; not grateful, but glad. The "Aunties" had arranged for a three-month, prepaid, room at the YWCA and a job at Serene Haven Nursing Home in Roxbury, a suitable choice, no doubt, given how thoroughly they had trained her to wait on other people.

On balance, Jadine's exhilaration at being free far outweighed her apprehension of the unknown. So what if she would celebrate her eighteenth birthday, in Boston, alone and unnoticed? That was fine with her.

The last thing Jadine did in Rochester was to mail a note addressed to Officer O'Day at the police station which read, *"A car with this license plate number has been seen in front of your house many, many afternoons. You'd better check it out."*

The morning "Auntie Stephie" drove Jadine to catch the early bus to Boston was as dark as nightfall. At the station, Jadine got out of the car, collected her belongings, and turned to wave just as "Auntie Stephie" quickly pulled away from the curb.

Thanks for nothing, you cheater.

An hour later, her face pressed against the bus window, she tried to see the deserted road ahead, unspooling like a black ribbon through the pummeling rain. Jadine wasn't sure what it was saying to her. She couldn't read it, but the farther she got from Rochester, the lighter she felt, as though she was molting layers of pain along the way.

"Don't forget about me," she whispered to herself, so that she could feel the heat of her breath. But she suspected that as soon as the bus was out of sight, no one in Rochester would notice her absence. It was the worst of fates—to be so easily forgotten.

What about Bear? Would she ever see him again? Or would he forget about her like everyone else she was leaving behind? In any case, she tried to convince herself not to feel guilty about what had happened to him.

After all, it had been his own doing.

CHAPTER SIXTEEN

With the introductory letter in hand, Jade waited to be interviewed by Ms. Obstrenski, the administrator of the Serene Haven Nursing Home. Cheryl, as she asked to be called, with her red, frizzy hair piled high on top of her head and her huge breasts that jiggled when she laughed, seemed so genuinely friendly that Jadine wasn't sure how to respond to her.

Right from the beginning, Jadine announced that she was to be called Jade, and Cheryl, saying, "sure, whatever floats your boat, Miss Tomecelli," had then led her on a tour of the facility, explaining that Serene was a convalescent nursing home and assisted living facility with rooms for thirty-five residents, some temporary, and some permanent. They passed a man doing a slow shuffle in scuffed slippers, cheeks furrowed over naked gums, and another man in a wheelchair, hanging from the seat like a toddler from his harness. Jade peeked into a bedroom where a woman, her shiny red lipstick leaking outside the lines of her mouth, waved at her.

Next, Cheryl turned into an activity room with a television, an upright piano, and several card tables stacked with games. There were about twelve patients lined up in chairs being led through arm and wrist exercises by a young woman who seemed suitably enthusiastic. The tour ended in the staff lounge which was outfitted with one long table and six chairs, a microwave sitting on the counter, a coffeemaker filled to the brim, and an older refrigerator bedecked with a sign reading "Cleanliness First." All the patients had seemed happy, Jade thought, as though they're being treated well.

According to Cheryl, Jade was to start by assisting the floor nurses wherever she was needed. Giving her a pastel-green cotton smock, as opposed to pink ones worn by volunteers, she told her to be there at seven the next morning. And that was it. She was about to begin her new life.

Walking out through the lobby, which was painted in bright primary colors, Jade was reminded of her old school, her *very* old school. When she had been there back in Dover, she would *never* have dreamed of ending up like this. Mama had wanted her to go to college, and here she was, lucky to have completed high school. Had she, Jade wondered now, ever stopped to consider what the impact of her departure would have on her daughter—that it might have catapulted her into a transient life of disdain and servitude? Which led to her wondering if Mama was still alive. Jade thought that if she had died, she would have felt some slight shift in the universe. But by now it had been so many years, she vowed to shrug off the lingering recriminations, to start out fresh, determined to forgive, albeit reluctantly.

Waiting for the bus to take her to the Y, she noticed that there was a small leafy park across the street from Serene, and knew right away that that was where she would spend lunch hours and coffee breaks. That was about the only thing she would miss about Rochester besides Bear; how she was able to take refuge in the woods where she could pretend she was someone special, not just plain Jadine Tomecelli, the orphan.

She missed Bear, terribly, remembering with a deep abiding pleasure of being with him, basking in his undivided attention. But, slowly, her expectation that she would always be with Bear had slipped away. Another person she had loved had disappeared. Yet hope was not linear, and the absence of a definitive answer still made her imagination jump and lurch as she concocted farfetched endings in which Bear, a decorated soldier, older, wiser, loving her as he always had, would return to explain that he hadn't written because he didn't want to make her feel that she had to waste years waiting for him. Or perhaps he'd been captured, held prisoner, and obviously could not write. She would run her finger down the long scar on his leg. They would kiss for a long, long time.

But daydreams were useless. She knew that. Think of all the time she had wasted imagining Mama's return. Perhaps the routine of work would be enough to drown her old fears in new hope. It wasn't her fault that Bear hadn't finished high school, the only goal that he had ever talked about. Bear had a temper. That's what had happened. He'd lost his temper. Or perhaps he was dead. From now on, she'd try to think the way that he had. She'd keep moving forward, and not blame anyone.

✳ ✳ ✳

That summer, during the first three months at Serene, Jade was the attendee of bedsores, the diaper changer, and the bedpan emptier, telling herself that the smell was no worse than chicken guts. It was not part of her job to take the pile of johnnies and towels to a Laundromat near the Y after work, but Jade had *offered* to do it for Cheryl. One thing she had learned over the last four years was that doing extra things for people could go a long way. Besides, this job was nothing compared to her chores with the "Aunties." And still, no one would ever know what she was thinking. She would hide herself from everyone. She knew now that that was the best protection.

She could only imagine what the "Aunties" may have said about her when they were lining up the job, but no one would get any information about her background out of Jade. She was friendly enough, but rarely spoke to the staff, unless asked a direct question. The patients often needed to be cheered up, and with them, she didn't need to talk about herself. Better to be a blank slate where there would be no trace of her old life in her new one. She did what was expected, and did it well. She needed this job and wasn't going to give Cheryl or other staff members any reason to get rid of her.

The room at the Y was merely a place to sleep, which didn't always come easily. Dreams plagued her, as they had ever since Mama had left, and she would often awake coated in sweat, her eyes prickling with tears, after nightmares in which tendrils of water lily stems threaded around her ankles, her wrists, her waist. As must have been the case with Angie, swirling water pulling her down, twisting around her like a sheet, the silky waterweeds clammy against her skin. Each time it was as frightening as the first.

One chilly September day, Jade sloshed through slanting silver ropes of rain on her way to work. She had just hung up her drenched raincoat and changed into her green smock and rubber-soled shoes, when Cheryl called her into the office.

"I really like the way you have immersed yourself in this job," she said, coming straight to the point. "That's why I'm offering you a chance to become a licensed practical nurse. I'll advance payment for you to take the LPN course at Roxbury Community College, with the understanding that you'll repay the loan by putting in extra hours here at Serene. The college is located over on Columbus Avenue, an easy walk from here. You're a natural, girl," she added with a huge smile. "Nurse Tomecelli—sounds right, don't you think?"

Every fiber of Jade's being focused on the task of not crying. This was a moment of kindness that threatened to break down all her defenses. She could feel the pressure behind her eyelids, at the base of her nose, in her jawbone, even at the edge of her ribcage. She hadn't cried since little Angie had died, and she was not going to now. Taking great care not to show any emotion except gratitude, she accepted the offer. But she was touched. So touched. No one had ever done anything for her "just because." Something from which only she would benefit.

And yet, despite her gratitude, she couldn't help wondering if Cheryl had an ulterior motive. Were suspicion and fear always going to be part of her life, she wondered? And if they were, would she ever be happy?

CHAPTER SEVENTEEN

W hen her pre-paid time at the Y was used up, Jade found a tiny month-to-month rental in a fourth floor walk-up tenement house on Huntington Avenue, and moved in with her few belongings including her precious retreat box with her braids, Mama's knitting needles, her purple scarf, and the little heart-shaped locket.

The studio had a plastered ceiling that was textured like cottage cheese, and stained by the smoke of long-extinguished cigarettes. Jade wasn't sure if the gray of the walls was from smoke or dirt, but was grateful that the room was furnished with the basics: a faded plaid slip-covered couch, a coffee table, a standing lamp, a bureau with a rusted fan on top, and a double bed on a low platform. The only thing she moved was a picture of Jesus with radiating rays of light behind His head, which she relegated to the back of the closet. She didn't need a picture of Him to guide her; she had only herself to depend on, and that would have to be enough.

When Jade touched the edge of one of the sheer curtains hanging in front of the only window in the apartment, it billowed with dust. Immediately taking them down, she scraped the grime off the window, using a knife to cut through the old paint that had sealed it shut. Even then, she was only able to open it about eight inches, which let a ribbon of cool air flow into the room. Dropping to the floor in front of the breeze, she sat for a long time, breathing in deep breaths, trying not to think too far ahead.

Once the LPN classes were underway, Jade doubled up on courses, determined to finish as soon as possible, studying like she never had before—first thing in the morning and last thing at night. Her lunch hour afforded time to study in the corner at the table in the staff lounge or in the park across from Serene. Her books were always open when she was on the bus—to and from work, to and from school. Fellow travelers did not jeer or comment the way they might have in Rochester. This was the big city, and she was anonymous. Besides, at least half of the other passengers were also students of some kind, cramming like crazy. No one took particular notice of her.

Beyond that, it was hard to plan. At least once a day she'd look up from her books and think about the fact that she was eighteen, legally an adult. She had no further ties with the New Hampshire DCYF and the "Aunties." All of that was history to be buried and forgotten. Besides, when they had arranged for the job with Serene, Jade was sure the "Aunties" had never dreamed that she would become anything more than a nurse's aide, emptying bedpans for a living. Feeling a little bit proud of herself made her study all the harder; not that she cared about proving them wrong. She needed to prove something important to herself—that she could be whatever she wanted to be.

Bear, I'm making it. How she would have liked to tell him.

Her landlord, Manny Ceruti, was a middle-aged drunk. Jade couldn't imagine how he had ever come to own the building because he seemed like a person who never worked a day in his life. Every Friday afternoon, Manny would drag a wooden chair from his first floor apartment into the front hall and sit, tilted back against a crumbling plaster wall among the large plastic garbage bags bulging with everybody's crap which he would put out in the morning, and there he'd be, waiting for his tenants to pay their weekly rent. Cash only. That was a laugh. As if any of his tenants had a checking account. He was not an inspiring sight, with the fly of his filthy chinos half open, holding a bottle in a brown paper bag in the crook of his arm.

Often, when she returned from work, it seemed as though he had been waiting for her, had just happened to be in the hall, holding the front door open. Sometimes he'd offer to carry her packages up to her room; other times he'd just stand there, always too close, leering. Jade never spoke to him no matter what he said to her. The pig. But she had no intentions of making waves. Finally having a place of her own meant too much to her for that.

✲ ✲ ✲

No one from Rochester ever called or wrote to her after she left except for pathetic Norma, the youngest Watson kid who had been her only ally during the six-month stay on their farm. Norma had sent Jade a postcard, care of Serene, saying merely, "I miss you." The card reminded Jade of her *assignment* with the Watsons—the *worst assignment by far*—living on that godforsaken farm with all those filthy, neglected animals. Especially the chickens. They had made *her* kill them—twist their necks until they were dead—and, after their lifeless bodies stopped jerking around in the dust of the dry barnyard, cut off their heads and then dunk their stinking, mite-infested bodies in scalding water to loosen their feathers so she could pluck them off. The first time Jeffrey Watson made her do it, she shrieked and then collapsed, which made "Auntie Lisa" come running. Screaming even louder, Jade had hoped to get him in trouble, but all she said to Jade was to get up and stop carrying on like a baby. For years, it came to her in all forms of nightmares, and there was no music, no birdsong, that could make it go away. That smell had made her gag. Even the memory of the smell made her gag.

Tearing Norma's postcard into tiny pieces, Jade had dropped it in the trash and poured herself a cup of coffee, listening to stray dogs fighting in the alley beneath her window.

As for Bear, although the memory of him never left her, he had faded to the back of her mind, where she had consciously forced any thoughts of him into a tiny capsule, small and inaccessible, along with Mama and Papa. And little Angie.

But that was then and now was now.

CHAPTER EIGHTEEN

All winter, bundled up against the cold and snow, Jade made her way to the Community College which was only a short walk in the evening from Serene, past wavering shadows of winter branches dancing on cement walls.

The instructors had told Jade that she had a gift for working with the elderly, although they warned her, as they did all their students, that they should take care not to become emotionally involved with the patients. That was, Jade told herself, something she was not likely to do. But they kept after her to smile, and she would, even though she was doing so on command.

Actually, Jade hated to be told to smile, and was determined that there would come a day when she'd smile only when she felt like it.

✤ ✤ ✤

The kind of phony persona her instructors wanted her to exude reminded Jade of her first year in Rochester High School and the January-June *assignment* with the

Johnson family. Both Georgia and Barry worked in sales
and they had told her repeatedly that she'd never get
anywhere with people if she didn't act friendlier, be more
open. Maybe that was the real clue—that relationships
were all an act. The six months with them had been
ridiculous, totally superficial. Jade had seen through
their phony crap in a heartbeat. They'd throw out a
question to her about school or whatever, and then turn
away before she had a chance to respond. Incredibly
fake. She'd never fallen for it. Not once.

"Auntie Georgia" had no idea that her own lying kids
were sneaking out at night and doing drugs. Jade had
never said a word about it. And she refused to smile, too.
What she *did* learn from them, however, she was putting
to use at Serene: to ask questions of her patients, show
interest, get them talking about themselves. And when
she'd leave their room, they'd know nothing about her,
except that they thought she was wonderful; this tall,
lovely-looking young woman who cared so deeply for
her patients.

As time went on, Jade found herself no longer
pretending. She *did* care. And that came as a complete
surprise.

One might have thought that it was just another
glorious spring day, but for Jade, it was the best day since
she had left Rochester, which now seemed a lifetime
ago. Not only had she completed all of her courses,
passed the licensing exam, and achieved her goal, but
all that studying had made her feel good about herself.
Now, she wanted to jump up and down and shout, "I
did it! I'm an LPN, a Licensed Practical Nurse!" She felt

dizzy and lighthearted, liking the sound of her new self. People would listen to Nurse Tomecelli, a triumphant, hard-working person who would command a real salary, real responsibility, not just someone who existed to take orders from people who despised her.

Finally, she would be shown some respect and give some orders of her own. The thought of it felt delicious.

Jade sat on her favorite stone bench in the park across from the nursing home, watching the silvery poplar leaves flutter against the sky. The fragrance from the sprig of purple lilacs, Mama's favorite flower that she had broken away from a nearby bush, was overwhelming. As she observed the pigeons waddling in the grass near her feet, pecking, ruffling their iridescent wings, she absently crushed the delicate blossoms, shredding them from their stems. When she stood, they fluttered to the ground and she wiped their scent from her hands against her pastel green cotton smock.

Too much beauty was still dangerous.

✻ ✻ ✻

After almost two years at Serene, Jade, now proudly wearing her white nurse's uniform, was assigned to the convalescent ward where a temporary patient, Josephine Gerard, was recuperating from a compound fracture of her right arm. When Jade first encountered her, she was sitting upright in her bed, wearing an old-fashioned bed-jacket, powder blue and lacey.

"Come on in, Jade," she said. "Isn't it a beautiful spring day?" The patient's full, rosy cheeks spread into a big smile.

And it was. Something about the woman touched a chord in Jade that made her, quite suddenly, aware of the golden branches of the forsythia bush just outside the window, glowing in the early morning sun.

"How are you feeling this morning, Mrs. Gerard?"

"Oh, please call me Josie, everyone does. Come sit by me a minute. I've been observing you ever since I came here. It's totally uncanny how you remind me of my daughter, Beatrice, who—well, she died in a car crash eight years ago. She was my only child," she added, taking a framed photograph off her nightstand and pressing it to her breast, weeping softly.

For sure, Mama never cried over losing me.

"Tell me about yourself, my dear," Josie asked, drying her eyes. "I'd like to know all about you." The patient leaned forward, trying to catch hold of Jade's hand.

"My life began here at Serene," Jade told her. "Before that, I was—I was an orphan. It's a part of my life I don't want to talk about. But please don't feel sad for me, everything is going great. I am happy." Jade stood, anxious to leave the room.

Josie seemed to understand. At least her expression was one of sympathy. But Jade could not help but wonder why she wanted to know so much about her. Was there, she wondered, something about that which should warn her to keep clear of this woman?

CHAPTER NINETEEN

That Friday had been the warmest day in June so far. The sun was just beginning to dip into the horizon when Jade left work. Stopping at Bruno's Grocery, she picked up a package of hotdogs, a loaf of bread, a small jar of applesauce and one of peanut butter, plus a couple of bananas. She was socking her money away and hated having to spend it on food. Actually, she didn't give a damn about food. She ate for energy—not hunger, or pleasure.

Even though she had been on her feet most of the day, Jade almost ran up the three flights to her apartment, eager to shower and relax. Inside was dark. She entered her room, using the old iron key, pulled the string for the bulb in the hall, threw back the curtain in the main room, and opened her window. Kicking off her shoes, she put the food away and took down the plastic Taster's Choice jar in which she stored her Friday "take." Serene's aides and nurses were not supposed to accept "tips" from the patients, but Jade decided that if they insisted, she would not object. Josie was the most generous.

Ever since she had been on her own, Jade indulged herself in long, hot showers, something she had never been allowed at any of her *assignments* in Rochester— wasteful and selfish, they had told her. Now, she'd turn the water on way ahead of time, letting it run while she undressed. Just as she reached for the faucet behind the plastic curtain, Jade smelled something disgusting— and familiar. Whipping the curtain back, there was her landlord, Manny, grinning, with one hand in her retreat box. Startled, he dropped the box and all the pieces of Jade's life bounced and skidded inside the tub. Stepping back from her, she heard something crunch beneath his foot.

How dare he sneak into my apartment, the filthy pervert.

Without even realizing what she was doing, only certain that she had to get him out of her private space, Jade picked up the plunger that sat next to the toilet, spun around, and with all her might, clobbered him on the side of his head. He slumped backwards; his body slowly collapsed. She stood there, trembling with fury, kindled by the instant recall of Ted Jenkins and his friends peeing on her, and how they got away with it. Climbing into the tub, a new surge of madness came over her, and she hit Manny with the plunger again. He never cried out. And strangely, she didn't either.

Leaning her head against the shower wall, she felt her blood beating in her ears and heard herself panting. She started to step out of the tub when, looking at his repugnant form, her wrath was so inflamed that she suddenly reached down, placed her hands on either side of his head, and with a quick move, twisted it until she heard his neck snap. Just like a chicken's, but much easier.

Straightening up, still straddling him, she felt the sweat pouring over her entire body. Holding her breath, she pushed hard until her breathing returned to normal. Now, all she could think of was to get his body out of her apartment. Stepping out of the tub, she reached back, grabbed his limp arms, and dragged him over the rim and across the bathroom floor, through the living room, and dropped him to the left of the door.

As she slipped on her robe, panic began to kick in, throbbing within her chest, spinning through her brain like a cyclone; a wave of adrenalin washed away every thought, except the question of how to get rid of him. Rushing to the kitchen, she banged into the edge of a table, and, gasping in pain, saw in the mirror that her pupils had receded to tiny black dots, and that her skin was so sallow that she was nearly unrecognizable.

Who is that person? she asked herself. Like Bear, had she just thrown over everything she had hoped for in one uncontrolled fit of rage? Standing flat against the counter, pinned there by shock, Jade took a glass down from the cabinet. The water gurgled in the pipes and splattered out in a rusty burst. She gulped it down, waiting for calm.

Listening at her door for sounds of activity in the hall, and hearing none, she quickly dragged the limp, foul-smelling body to the top landing, curled him in a fetal position, and rolled him down the stairs to the second floor. She followed, pushing him to keep up the momentum. She stood motionless for a moment, listening—no one appeared, so she dragged him to the top of the next stairwell, and with another mighty push, sent him tumbling down, where he landed among the trash bags in the front hall.

Still barefooted, Jadine scrambled back up the stairs, ran into her apartment, where, going to the kitchen, she poured liquid detergent onto her hands and stood there scrubbing her skin raw despite the fact that she knew that, for her at least, the smell of that man would never go away. Her hair, now past her shoulders, sprang curls in the sweat around her face. She combed it back with her wet fingers.

Only then did she remember her retreat box. Rushing into the bathroom, Jade found what the landlord had stepped on . . . her mother's locket, the hinge snapped apart. Gathering the rest of her mementos from the tub, she quickly dropped them back into the box, placing the cover on firmly. *Not now. She couldn't think about it yet. She needed to check the entire bathroom.* Amazingly, she told herself, there was no blood there and none anywhere else in her apartment. She hadn't remembered seeing any on the stairs, either.

Suddenly overcome with the feeling of her own weight settling, of everything around her dropping into slow motion, Jade stood as if frozen in place in the middle of the room. She couldn't believe what she had just done—*killed a man.* But it was self-defense. Only, she'd worked so hard these past two years, she prayed, oh God, she prayed that she wouldn't be connected to his death. The way things had gone in her life, no one would believe that she was defending herself. She wasn't a coldblooded killer. She did things only when backed into a corner. She did what anyone would have done, given the same proclivity for quick thinking . . . it's not as if she enjoyed it. It wasn't recreational.

She couldn't say how much time passed before she heard a man in the hallway, shouting for someone to call 911. Taking a deep breath, Jade pulled open her door and joined the other tenants who were staring down, unsympathetically, at the twisted body of their former landlord.

"What's going on? What happened?" She made her voice join the other tenants'.

And all that Jade could think was that this was *his* fault. That he had brought it on himself.

CHAPTER TWENTY

H er chart had a notation that Mrs. Gerard could only be discharged if she had someone looking out for her at home. Jade had known this for several days and was sure that Josie was working her way around to asking her. *It could be a perfect solution.* Although the police had declared Manny's death accidental due to having fallen down the stairs in a state of extreme intoxication and broken his neck, she was desperate to move out of that building.

The place had taken on a smell that wouldn't go away no matter how much she cleaned. Perhaps, she thought, it was the smell of fear. In any case, the apartment was cursed for her now, a constant reminder that she had actually killed a man—ended his life in a violent way. She found herself replaying those terrible minutes until she had extracted from them every possible nugget of meaning. If she had done nothing, what would have happened to her? Something much worse than what happened after Ted Jenkins had thrown her to the ground and the boys peed on her. Until Bear had come along, she had been defenseless then, but this time, there had been no Bear.

"My dear Jade," Josie said, finally approaching the subject that afternoon, "I'm ready to go home, but they don't think I should be alone, and frankly, I agree. If you would be willing to move in with me, you would have your own room and the use of my car. I'm feeling stronger every day. I know I wouldn't be a lot of work for you."

She was so eager that her words were stumbling over one another. "Please Jade, you would be free to come and go whenever you want. You—you'd be . . ." her voice faltered. "You'd be just like Beatrice, like a daughter to me."

Jade knew better than to take the bait at once. She'd lived in other people's houses before and this time she wanted to be wooed.

"Oh, please," Josie said, touching her arm. "I will have to go to physical therapy for a while, but after that, you'll have all kinds of free time to pursue your nursing career or whatever you want to do."

"Well, would I have my own room?"

"Yes, my dear. It's just the same way as before my Bea died. I haven't touched a thing in her room."

"I don't know . . ."

Up till now, everything in her life had been like a million scattered pieces of a puzzle that she had been searching through just to find two that would fit together, a starting place, a handhold. Maybe this was it—the first two pieces that seemed to fit. She and Mrs. Gerard.

"There's one condition," Jade said, dropping her voice to a whisper. "As long as we do *not* tell Cheryl what we're doing. It will be our secret. As far as she would know, I will have just quit working here, and you'll have arranged for a personal healthcare person on your own. You see, my privacy is very important to me. Will you promise, absolutely, not to tell a soul?"

Josie hesitated, but only a moment, before opening her arms to Jade, who took hold of her outstretched hands and shook them firmly.

No hugging. No getting involved emotionally.

"Tell them at the desk that you have arranged for home care, and that a taxi will pick you up at eleven on a Saturday," Jade told her. "That's Cheryl's day off. I'll already have given the driver instructions about picking me up at my apartment. You will have to sign yourself out. Are you all right with this plan?"

Josie nodded enthusiastically.

Perhaps, Jade thought, such subterfuge was unnecessary, but you could never tell. The important thing was that she protected herself.

✵ ✵ ✵

Dear Cheryl,

I cannot tell you how much I appreciate what you have done for me over the last two years at Serene. Unfortunately, I have been called, as an emergency, to go to Canada to attend my dying mother. I am so sorry that there was not enough time for me to give the proper notice. PLEASE BELIEVE ME, I have every intention of paying you back, in full, for the money you laid out for my training. Yours was the best vote of confidence that has ever been offered to me and I want you to know how much it meant.

Good luck and I hope you will always think of me kindly.
Sincerely,
Jadine Tomecelli

Around seven that Friday evening, Jade signed her brief letter, sealed the envelope, and slipped it under Cheryl's door. She knew Cheryl would be shocked and no doubt angry; not only because she had trusted her, but because the schedule would have to be completely reworked. But that was beside the point now. Scheduling was one of Cheryl's biggest headaches. *She might even go over to Huntington Avenue and check out her rental . . . ask questions of the other tenants.*

Cheryl would hit a stone wall, Jade thought, since she didn't believe that the other tenants there even knew her *first* name because she seldom, if ever, spoke to anyone. Not taking any chances though, Jade decided to tell at least one person there that she was off to Canada.

Heading up the stairs to clean out her room, Jade recognized a woman who lived on the second floor. "Hi, my name is Tomecelli. I live upstairs."

"Yeah? And so?"

"Well, I thought I should tell someone in the building that I'm leaving. My mom is dying in Canada and I'm going to stay with her. You know, take care of her."

"What's that got to do with me?"

"I guess I thought someone should know. My rent's paid up and I'll leave the place clean."

"Okay, so you told someone. Good luck to your mother. None of my kids give a shit about me."

With that seed planted, Jade continued up the stairs to pack and leave that dump forever. A film closed over her past as she moved around her despised lodgings, a barrier as brittle and fragile as ice forming. It grew to become impenetrable, opaque.

Her last night there, Jade had a terrible dream. She was lying on a small bed in a room she had never seen before, in a house that wasn't hers, hands and feet bound, shaking with terror as the dark silhouette of a man came to stand next to her bed, and there was a woman watching, smiling—a woman who looked a lot like Beaknose.

Or Mama.

When she awoke, shaken, she was sure it had been Mama.

CHAPTER TWENTY-ONE

As she got out of her taxi, Jade knew Josie was watching closely for her reaction as she proudly stood in front of her clapboard Colonial. In the rush to accept her offer, Jade had neglected to ask where she lived and was relieved when she heard it was in a lovely residential part of Brookline, which was just enough removed from Huntington Avenue Apartments and Serene Haven Nursing Home to make her feel that she would be safe from detection there. All of the houses in Josie's neighborhood were neat, well-groomed, and, although obviously developed by the same builder, each one reflected the taste of its owner. The sidewalks on both sides of the street were lined with linden trees; their dense, heart-shaped leaves seemed to be welcoming them.

Josie's house was yellow with black shutters, looking just a little neglected, especially the landscaping. I can do something about that, Jade thought, looking at the stunted rhododendrons and the scrappy lawn, remembering her very first *assignment*, which had been with the Dombroski family when she was fourteen.

She had spent all of her free time that summer and fall working in their yard while their spoiled-rotten daughter, Annette, although she was the same age as Jade, rode her bike around the neighborhood, hanging out with her friends. "Auntie Evelyn" had stood over Jade, instructing her as to how and where to plant flowers in front of the house and how to turn over the earth to prepare for a "kitchen" garden at the back. "No, not that way, Jaydeen." *She could hear her voice now.* "Can't you do anything right?"

She hated me. Forget it, it was mutual.

Never before had Jade admitted, though, that she had actually enjoyed working in the garden, particularly since now, at Josie's house, she could do it her own way. Zinnias, daisies, lily-of-the-valley, and especially a purple smoke tree. Of course she'd confer with Josie first.

Jade turned to Josie and watched the soft down of her white hair play about her scalp like a half-blown dandelion. She could feel the older woman's need reaching out like a terrible vine, wrapping itself around her, and was surprised to discover that she didn't resent it. The "Aunties'" need for her labor had been cold and calculating, exploiting her, but this felt different because she now had a choice.

They entered the front hall, where steep stairs rose to the bedrooms above. The afternoon light filtered through the thin curtains in a pleasant glow. The wallpaper, soft pink roses on trellises, was faded but in good condition. Although the air was the kind of musty that comes with a house closed up for almost eight weeks, Jade felt a surge of warmth within its walls run through her body; a kind of acceptance, like coming home after a long absence, offering an unimaginable future, ticking along in time, vessels carrying her to her own destiny.

"Where do you sleep, Josie?"

"Upstairs, first door on the right," she said, running her hand over the newel post of dark wood, polished smooth and bright. "I—I want you to have Bea's room across from mine."

There was a look of such hopefulness that Jade turned away, embarrassed, unsure.

What does she want from me? It was a question that it seemed she always had to ask herself.

Bea's room, undisturbed for years other than the daily swipe of sunlight across the mirror, was somehow welcoming to Jade; sort of like what she pictured her own room might have been had her life not taken one ugly turn after another. She placed her retreat box on a shelf in the closet; the only new addition to her memory treasures was her nurse's pin, which she no longer needed to wear.

CHAPTER TWENTY-TWO

They soon fell into a comfortable rhythm, Josie becoming more and more dependent on Jade for all of the food shopping, banking, and other errands. Having taken driver's education in high school, but never having obtained her license, Jade now drove with extreme caution without one. After observing Josie's physical therapy sessions twice, she decided she could just as well save Josie that expense and become her therapist herself.

Josie had told her that money was no object, but that meant little to Jade for whom scrimping had been a way of life. When Josie asked her to take over the checkbook, Jade was surprised, but pleased. She decided to cut back on their expenses. There were, after all, a lot of things Josie could do without, like delivered meals from The Gourmet Café, and she wanted nothing for herself. Where she got this sense of how to handle money was a bit of a mystery, but Jade knew that she did it well and Josie never questioned her.

"You've grown into such a beautiful young woman, Jadie. Don't go falling in love and leave me," Josie often teased her, to which Jade replied that there was no need for her to worry since she simply didn't have the time.

And Jade meant what she said. That always reassured her, Jade thought with a laugh, as if she would ever be interested in the kind of love that Mama had had for Papa. *There was only one kind of love, and that went out of her life along with Bear.* Besides, the *assignment* with the Nicholsons and their wonderful son, Al Junior, had taught her a painful lesson. At their house, she had slept on a cot, sharing the adorable, pink bedroom with their "surprise" daughter, Allyson, who was eleven years younger than she and Junior. No matter where Jade had been in their house or what she had been doing, she had felt Junior's eyes follow her, and even more so at school where he would rush to walk beside her in the hallways, possessively draping his arm around her shoulder.

"Cut it out, Junior," she had told him every time, shrugging his arm away. She could still remember how uncomfortable it had made her feel. Was it because she hated any kind of show of affection, or had she been afraid that Bear might see them. Was that why?

It had been no more than six weeks into this *assignment*, when Junior had actually told her that he thought he was falling for her. At first, she had just laughed at him and pushed him away. But he had hounded her; wouldn't let up with the compliments, the sneaky attempts to touch her, until one cold day in March, on the pretense of needing to talk to her about something serious, he had lured her into the back seat of the Toyota parked in the garage. He had immediately tried to run his hand under her sweater. Shoving him back, really hard, Jadine had a sudden vision of her Mama smacking Papa and saying viciously, "Don't!" when he had come up behind her in the kitchen once, wrapping his arms around her, cupping her breasts in both hands. The memory had come back so vividly, it made her squeeze her eyes to shut it out.

Because nothing ever went right in her life, that was when dear little sister Allyson, who hated sharing her room with "Jadine, the nanny," discovered them in the car, and tattled.

"Jadine won't leave me alone," Junior had whined to his parents. "She's constantly begging to be with me."

Standing in the hall outside Junior's room, she had heard the boy who was so madly in love with her, who would do anything for her if she would only let him kiss her, sell her down the river. *God, how she hated boys.* If that was romance, she told herself, she could do without it forever.

Without listening to her side of what had happened, "Auntie Connie" had told her never to speak to Junior again, for any reason. That was fine with her.

"I don't want you to even be in the same room with Al Junior," she said. "Am I making myself clear? That means whether you're eating or doing homework or chores around the house. Do you understand?"

Jadine had been glad enough to agree, particularly since she had made up her mind to never speak to any of the Nicholson family again except when absolutely necessary, and then in monosyllables. She hoped they would burn in hell—all of them.

Some time later, a stash of pot was found in Junior's locker at school, which resulted in his being suspended for two weeks and kicked off the football team, which in turn made him lose the scholarship to U. Mass. And then, mysteriously, his senior term paper seemed to have gotten lost, even though he swore to God that he had written it and had put it in his locker.

Jade figured he had gotten a small portion of what he'd deserved.

Josie was looking doubtfully at her, but it was true—she was not interested in love. Sometimes, in line at the grocery store, Jade glanced at the headlines of the women's magazines: *"How to Hook a Man."* She had no desire to pick up the magazine and read further. Wasn't that what Beaknose had done to Papa? Got him hooked? Jade could not consider putting another human being through the kind of childhood she'd suffered. How could she ever be sure she would not do something like Mama had done if she ever married and had a child?

Besides, she was falling in love, if that's what this emotion was, with Josie. When she'd told her about wanting to work in the garden, Josie's eyes had sparkled.

"Would you be able to bring the garden back to life?" she'd asked.

"There's a nursery down Route 9," Jade told her. "I was thinking of going to buy some plants. Some rose bushes? What are your favorite colors, Josie?"

"Yellow. As you can see, that's the color I chose for my house. Get whatever you want, dear. I'm sure it'll be wonderful."

To have her wishes granted and confidence bestowed in one breath was almost more than Jade could handle.

Mornings, there were eggs, sunny-side up; the whistling kettle; buttered toast. She discovered the pleasure of sitting peacefully with another person over a meal, exchanging ideas and making plans. Josie's familiar gestures as she spoke; the quiet request to pass the jelly or salt; their attentive conversation about how the day would unfold. All of this was new to Jade. She was saddened to realize she'd lived her whole life without it. Simply having someone else *care* whether she'd slept well, filled Jade with a joy she did not trust. Because surely Josie would eventually tire of her. She'd forget the strawberries or wreck her car and then Josie would turn against her. This state of grace must be merely temporary. Another *assignment* would come along, and this happiness would all end.

The day came when Jade, planting tulip bulbs in the side yard, forgot about the chicken roasting in the oven. She didn't even hear Josie's call, the two-syllable word she made from her name: Ja-die, Ja-die.

The smoke alarm was ringing, the kitchen filled with smoke. Jade felt her heart pounding as she rushed to turn off the oven, open windows, and deactivate the alarm.

"Oh Josie, I'm so sorry," she cried. "How can you ever forgive me?"

I knew this would happen. Nothing lasts. See? Now Josie knows. I can't do anything right, not even cook a decent meal. And here I am living in her house, still a failure, with nowhere to go and nothing to call my own.

So absorbed was she in regret that she barely felt Josie's hand on her shoulder.

"Jadie, dear," she said, "we all make mistakes. It could happen to anyone. Besides, I was the one who fell asleep. If my hearing was better I would have heard the bell go off. If my sense of smell was better I would have smelled it myself. Let's use this as an excuse to eat out tonight. Shall we?"

Jade nodded, her face streaked with garden soil, and all she could think was, *she isn't angry? She doesn't want to get rid of me?* So used to criticism and "consequences" for unacceptable behavior, Jade now felt a rush of relief and gratitude so intense, it made her tremble.

"Why don't you go take a shower, dear," Josie added. "We can take care of this mess later."

Jade stood under the water for a long time. When she dressed and was finally sitting across from kind, kind Josie, both of them digging into heaping servings of Caesar salads, she didn't think she'd ever been so clean, or so content.

CHAPTER TWENTY-THREE

During the following year, Jade matured in many ways, finding herself able to take control of any situation, something she knew pleased most older people, and at the same time, having genuine concern for the details of Josie's well-being. Josie, who constantly craved affection. That had been the hardest part for her at Serene—showing fondness in a convincing way. But Josie's affection for her was so genuine that it was gradually breaking the barriers she had set against feeling attached to anyone.

"I don't dream of Bea anymore," Josie commented one morning over breakfast, "just you, my dear Jadie. You are like my daughter."

Jumping up from the table to retrieve marmalade from the refrigerator, Jade lowered her head until her straight chestnut hair fell across her cheekbones hiding her hazel eyes that could be as soft as smoke or as hard and cold as a rock.

"I am nobody's daughter," she replied. "Nobody's."

"Why do you keep saying that, Jadie?" Josie protested. "Talking about your past could help you let go of unhappy memories, you know."

"I told you before. I have no memories, good or bad," Jade muttered. Pulling the corduroy chair cushion from behind her back, she stroked it like the pelt of a cat.

"You *are* my daughter now," Josie told her. "I love you, Jade Tomecelli. Does that mean anything to you?"

There was a beat of silence while Jade's fear rushed at her from every direction.

"Yes, it does," she admitted, her hand once again moving back and forth over the cushion. "It actually makes me very happy."

The admission would be fatal, Jade knew this. Josie had seen her hesitation, and now it was too late to take it back. *Although, this could be what she had been missing her whole life.*

Josie smiled triumphantly, and hiked her chair closer to Jade's.

"I've been thinking a lot about something," she said in a low voice. "We've been together a year now, and you are still saying that you're an orphan. It hurts my heart every time you say it."

Her voice slipped into the silence that followed, like a stone through water, quick and smoothly appeasing.

"Well, I'm just going to come right out with it," Josie went on. "I want to adopt you, Jade. Make you officially my daughter. Jade Gerard. Doesn't that sound perfect?"

Jade could hear herself breathe, a deep rushing sound through her nostrils. *This couldn't be happening to me. What would Bear tell me to do?*

"Have you lost your mind?" she demanded.

"No. It's the best idea I've had in years," Josie said. If she was hurt, she did not show it.

"Why would you want to do such a thing?"

Her offer brought back that hollowed-out feeling of original loss so intensely that Jade discovered that she could not meet her eyes.

"Because I don't want you to say, ever again in your life, that you're an orphan. Be my daughter, Jade. Please, say yes."

Feeling as though her world had suddenly become fragile, Jade stood abruptly and held on to the counter to steady herself. Outside the kitchen window, she could see mourning doves step gingerly across the grass, their heads bobbing in the manner of wise men, their throaty coos speaking of safety and peace. Looking back at Josie, she heard in her mind the dark distant roar of the past.

The quiet pulsed between them for a long moment before she found her voice.

"You are too good to me," she whispered, longing to bridge the distance between them, the distance she had so carefully created. Because she couldn't possibly love me, she thought, even as Josie was saying that she did.

CHAPTER TWENTY-FOUR

Finally grown out since his days of wearing a severe military brush-cut, Bear's black hair was slicked straight back from his face, the same way he had worn it in high school. At six-three now, and one hundred and eighty pounds, every bit of it lean, hard muscle, he had changed into manhood.

In the beginning, he had felt like killing someone. Anyone. The army was not what he had wanted, nowhere close to his plan especially since he was certain that Jade had come to trust him, finally. And then, suddenly, that ass-kissing principal who refused to believe what really had happened that vile day in the woods, had separated him from the only person in the world he had ever cared about.

Although he hadn't given a shit about saying goodbye to the Bidwells—punching that bastard out would've been more like it—he wasn't even allowed to go back to the farm for his belongings. Not that there had been anything much of value there, but he could at least have been able to see the animals one last time, maybe open the gates and set them free.

There had been an exact moment of resolve for Bear when he had been locked in the brig for drunken brawling during basic training, and then, waking to a vicious headache and a split lip, he had vowed to make something of himself—something he could be proud of. If he was going to take care of Jade, he had to *be* somebody and stand for something important. So, during those six transitional years, Lieutenant Billy-John Kuruk, better known as Bear, had taken advantage of every opportunity the army had to offer. Not only had he finished high school, he had acquired training in law enforcement. All on the taxpayers' tab.

The strict regime of military life had been easy for him after the privations he had suffered at The Home: every day there was a structured routine of meals, and then all ages in the same classroom until they were marched to the parking lot, which doubled as a playground, no matter what the weather, until 5:00 pm— all of which were reasons, ironically, why Bear had done so well in the army. Furthermore, thanks to his excellent eye-hand coordination, a steady aim, and an easy trigger pull, he had ranked high in marksmanship, which was why he had been assigned to Military Police duty instead of the infantry. A matter of aptitude, they had said. This was how he could best defend his country. It had not been a difficult task for an angry young man.

Since leaving the service with an excellent recommendation from Uncle Sam, Bear was able to choose between several civilian job openings. The army had given him discipline, a sense of honor and justice, and the desire to build a better life for himself. Now that he was out of the army, he vowed to find Jade and protect her. They would have a life together. There was no question in his mind that he could make that happen.

Within two years of serving in the Winthrop Police Department, he had landed his first choice—the Boston Homicide Division—all the while, he had searched for Jade, starting with Serene Haven Nursing Home in Roxbury.

"She left her job here quite suddenly," Cheryl Obstrenski had told him. "That was years ago, but I do remember that there was a note from her about going to Canada to care for her ailing mother."

"She never contacted you after that?" Bear asked.

"No. That's all I can tell you, except that she did send me a money order, almost a year later, to cover the cost of her nurses' training."

"So, she's a nurse?"

"Yes, and a damn good one, at that. She was a natural, and in spite of how disappointed I was in her for leaving so abruptly, I'll always remember her that way."

Bear thanked Cheryl and left his card just in case she ever heard from Jade again, after which he contacted all the hospitals and nursing homes in the Boston area, but without success. And there were no Tomecelli's listed in the phonebook.

What haunted him the most was, why hadn't she answered his letters making plans for them to meet right after she graduated? *Why?*

He was at a dead end. Jadine Tomecelli seemed to have vanished.

CHAPTER TWENTY-FIVE

Arriving in Boston in February with two duffle bags and a small suitcase, Bear went straight to Fourth Street where he had set up an appointment to look at a small, one-bedroom apartment. The house was set in the middle of a row of gray clapboard triple-decker homes tucked behind covered front porches, all with small yards delineated by mature maples. The real estate agent led him through one of the two entry doors, and up to the third floor, telling him that if he stood in the corner of the living room and tipped his head to the right, he could see, far in the distance, a sliver of blue through the roofs of the thickly settled neighborhood. "That's ocean view, son," he quipped.

Less than five minutes of looking around and Bear knew, even without the agent's sales pitch, that this place was to become his new home. Actually, the first real one he had ever had of his own, since no one would count that room he had lived in for two years in Winthrop.

Bear felt completely content living in respectable poverty because, even though it was a rental, it was all his. He liked the main room especially, the bay windows and ten-foot ceilings, even though they were marred with water stains, as dark as thunderclouds.

That had been almost two years ago, and he'd never considered moving. He had accumulated all of the necessities for apartment living, mostly at the Salvation Army, which was only an eight-block hike from his place. Although he usually ate on the fly, there was a variety store at the end of Fourth Street where he could pick up a few basics. Faneuil Hall was also within a reasonable distance, and interesting to look around in, but too expensive for someone on a detective's salary.

Feeling at home in Boston, he liked walking past the Vietnamese restaurants that dotted his neighborhood, side-by-side with Irish pubs decorated with green shamrocks, and he liked the way the native Bostonians drew out the first syllable. And then there was the cosmopolitan atmosphere created by hearing Spanish, Creole, French, all spoken in the streets. But he particularly liked the Irish brogue that O'Malley at the station put on when he told jokes. Diversity and anonymity. That's the way he wanted to live his life.

While in Winthrop, a fellow detective had introduced Bear to the idea of saving toward the future, so he opened an investment account and acquired the habit of consistently depositing one third of each paycheck into a variety of mutual funds, which was just one of the factors that made him prize his independence. He had no desire to interact with his neighbors and seldom even saw them because of the odd hours he kept. Since he wasn't required to wear a uniform, they probably had no idea what he did for a living. And that was the way he liked it.

Jade would be the final touch to this picture, living together, making a life—a life that it seemed he now had to follow without her.

☆ ☆ ☆

Yvonne Garneau, the dispatcher at the station, knew where everyone was at any given moment. She wasn't being nosy; it was her job to know. Bear had been aware of her friendliness from the first week he'd joined the Boston squad. Although she was nothing like the Jade he remembered, he was aware that Yvonne was a pretty girl, petite with honey-blonde hair that curled appealingly around her oval face, and that she seemed to be the type who needed someone to look out for her, which made him feel a little uncomfortable. Even though Yvonne had never come on to him in an offensive way, she just always seemed to be *there* whenever he ate lunch at his desk or when he was leaving for the day. She was likable enough, but he sure as hell didn't want his reaction to be mistaken for anything more than amicable. He'd had plenty of experience with girls during his six years in the army, drunken days on leave, and some in Winthrop—nights not to be remembered— although those encounters meant little to him since, after leaving Jade, he was detached from romantic emotions, as though something had died inside him.

Every morning, well before dawn, Bear ran at least six miles, taking off from Fourth Street, navigating the curvy back streets to Savin Hill, then down to the Waterfront . . . a lone figure silhouetted against the horizon. Staying in shape was just as important to him as the solitude of his run, his senses sharpened by the silence of the city at that hour. It was then when he felt most alone that he was bedeviled by the memories of the girl he had left behind.

CHAPTER TWENTY-SIX

"That one told me, 'Give me money! Don't move,'" Rudy Sharad explained excitedly to Bear and his partner, Lappas, pointing at the man on the floor as he stood in the bulletproof enclosure of his Community Meat and Grocery store on Tremont Street. "But, I moved. Very quick, I moved."

Witnesses reported to the detectives that, without any hesitation, Sharad had grabbed his .32 caliber pistol, come out from behind his protection, crouched, and shot. The other robber had fled, firing back wildly as he ran.

"I was wiping the lotto-card scratchings from the counter," Sharad continued quickly, "when these two men in ski masks and hooded shirts dashed through the front door. One raised a revolver to my face as the other one headed for the cooler—the third robbery since I opened last fall. This time," he added proudly, "I was ready."

Bear thought of the little grocery store where he often shopped. Only a week ago, he'd advised the owner to put in a safe and a silent alarm, clear his front window for easier observation, and increase the lighting in his parking lot. Some stores, he had told him, had put in electronic door locks, connected to a buzzer behind the register.

"No matter what I do, the robberies don't stop," Sharad told Lappas while Bear looked around the store.

"Shot him right through the heart," the medical examiner, who was just finishing up with the victim, told Bear. "Died almost instantly. These crooks just don't seem to learn. See that gun over there, next to the guy's hand? If Mr. Sharad had not gotten off a shot, there would be no storekeeper."

Bear nodded.

Meanwhile, the owner, folding his arms across his chest, almost defiantly, declared, "I didn't want to kill any people, but they wanted to kill me."

"We're only a phone call away," Lappas reminded him.

"Hey, I'm just trying to make a living. I have a family, you know."

That was always what happened, Bear thought. There was always the excuse, and it was never, ever anyone's fault.

✲ ✲ ✲

Years of investigating homicides had taught Bear to mask his feelings. In order to do the kind of job he knew a situation demanded, he had developed an ability to conceal his emotions to the extent that the other detectives in the squad all agreed that they'd never known anyone less bothered by a homicide victim. Bear had been amused when he had once overheard his partner saying, "He'd get right down there with the bloody corpse, checking like you'd check a dog for fleas. Nothing seems to affect the guy."

The truth was that that was the only way he knew to properly conduct an investigation. In their minds, however, he was a renegade because, although he had a remarkable record for solving cases, he never seemed weary of running down blind alleys.

Expect the worst and you'll never be disappointed was his motto.

Bear knew too well the danger of stepping beyond that fine emotional line. Pretend it isn't real, he constantly reminded himself; do your job, and keep your distance. If you start caring, it affects your judgment—although it was still hard to understand how a mother could murder her own child, *or put it in a laundry basket and leave it next to the trash in the middle of winter.* There was no sleep sound enough to erase the scenes of horror that had been burned inside his mind's eye, or his imagination.

When Mike Lappas was first assigned to be his partner, Bear had objected strenuously, citing that his application had been strictly for solo work. He would, he said, never entrust his life to anyone. But the assignment stood, and he was stuck with lean, wiry Lappas, who kept his black curly hair so long that he had to wear it in a ponytail to satisfy police force requirements, and who was younger, less experienced, and way too anxious to become a buddy.

Now and then, Bear would give in to Lappas' plea that they catch a *real* Italian meal at La Primavera in the North End where "they've got the greatest manicotti in all Bean Town, and Sangria by the pitcher."

"What more could you want?" he'd always add.

"Not much," Bear would sometimes say, and off they would go.

Occasionally, Yvonne would just happen along when they were leaving and, of course, Lappas would invite her to join them. Bear hoped that the attraction was his partner and not himself, because he would find it difficult to explain to anyone interested in a serious relationship with him that he had long since been taken.

✡ ✡ ✡

One night, a few months later, Bear was alone in The Brown Derby, one of his favorite sports bar, which he had chosen because it was just out of his district. It was similar to most every bar he had ever been in, with one large room and a half dozen TV screens on the walls or hanging from the ceiling, all tuned to sports channels. The Monday night football game was on, and he'd been drinking all evening. Drunk. *Oh, shit, was he drunk.* Looking around, the people seemed like shadows, sitting in small groups at round tables, or standing pressed along the long dark counter. The place smelled like urine and smoke and spilled beer.

Halftime, and suddenly Bear's attention was drawn to a highly made-up, quaffed, plastic-looking woman on the TV, reporting on Native American youth, her annoying voice carrying above the muffled roar of the drinkers around him:

" . . . *they suffer from child abuse and neglect, foster homes, school problems and dropouts, peer relation effects, family modeling response, fetal alcohol syndrome, developmental factors, and, most importantly, social deprivation."*

"Jesus, those stupid savages are in big trouble," Bear blurted out, his words slurred and pugnacious. Looking down the bar, he tried to catch the eye of some person who would engage—he wanted to argue with someone, anyone. "Those red-men are public health problem number one, a threat to society," Bear declared, pounding his fist on the bar. "Those fuckers should be sent back where they came from."

Someone tapped him on the shoulder, probably a bouncer, or maybe even an off-duty cop. "Clam it up, mister," he said.

"... *five times more likely than whites to die of alcohol-related causes ... higher rates of drunk driving ...*"

"Hey, buddy," Bear said, turning to the man at his elbow, "if you're a cop, you'd better get your ass out and nail those drunk Injuns," Bear gave him a loose smile and tried to put his arm around his shoulder. "They are the worst offenders."

In one second, the bouncer had Bear's arm twisted behind his back. "Cool it, mister, or you're out of here," he muttered.

"... *where are the buffalo today, and what's become of the vast land that was once their cherished home?*"

"Yeah. Where are the buffalo?" Bear shouted, scanning the room for an answer.

"... *highest rates of fetal alcohol syndrome in the nation ...*"

"Oh my God, that's what happened ... me Madre was a boozer! There's no help for me, I was obviously born drunk—"

"Okay mister, you're done," the bouncer said. "Pay up and get out."

The reporter's voice kept going. Bear wondered why they didn't turn her off— shut that bitch the hell up.

The next thing Bear knew, he was being escorted out of the bar and shoved into a cab. What seemed like only minutes later, he was being half-pushed, half-dragged up a flight of stairs. And then it was morning, and there was Yvonne offering him coffee and a fresh towel, and asking him if he wanted to take a shower.

Sweet Jesus, how the hell did I end up in her apartment? Bear mumbled to himself as he turned the shower on, full cold. Christ, he hadn't gone off the deep end like that in so long that he thought maybe he had conquered it, but the old familiar anger came over him so quickly at times—the feeling that he was going to explode. The goddamn stupid reporter blabbing away during halftime had set him off. No—let's face it—he'd already been shitfaced. Maybe the report was true and did relate to him, though; maybe he *had* been born drunk. He had sat there in the bar embedded in his anger, learning as everyone does, that old hatreds are endlessly retrievable. But what about Yvonne? He forced himself to consider her. Where the hell had she come from? She'd just seemed to materialize out of thin air. How had she discovered The Brown Derby, his secret place to let down and let go? No doubt she had wormed it out of Lappas who, although he knew that Bear went there occasionally, had never joined him.

How did she get him up the stairs to her apartment? He didn't remember anything much after midway through that evening. He had stayed aloof of any serious involvement with women all these years . . . now that resolve seemed irrevocably altered, and he worried that she was bound to be a problem. He could no longer picture himself acting natural in Yvonne's presence even though she had simply laughed it off.

"Don't worry, Billy-John, you're still a virgin," she had said just before he left her apartment.

All his life he had been a stranger to himself.

CHAPTER TWENTY-SEVEN

Christmas again. Carrying the decorations up from the basement, Jade admitted to herself that living with Josie—being her daughter—had totally changed everything. She could hardly believe that five years had passed since the adoption was legalized. Never having signed any kind of contract before that momentous event—not for a car, not for an apartment, not for anything—she'd found herself doing something that would be binding forever. It had terrified her, even though she knew it was an opportunity that would never come again. Josie had offered Jade a giant step away from the past.

Immediately afterward, she had applied for a social security number and a driver's license under her new name, *Jade Gerard*. A savings account and a credit card had put the final seal on her new identity. At first, it had seemed almost like a charade. However, it hadn't taken long, after the arrangements were completed, for her to recognize not only the benefits, but that, to her amazement, she was feeling toward Josie something much more than gratitude. She loved her, and oh, it felt so good.

Yet the past was still no further away than her dreaded dreams, even though they came much less frequently now. She winced at the memory of what had happened, things she had done, and tried to put them out of her mind. Whether it was the series of events that started with little Angie or the punishment of her despised landlord—all that had begun to seem less real, more like something she had fantasized—so that instead of being stuck there, she could go on, and by the grace of God, and Josie, lead her new life, undestroyed by what she truly believed had *not* been her doing.

Now, six years since Serene, Jade ran the household; cleaned, cooked, and took care of Josie's physical needs, and they were both thriving. Jade believed that whatever she was doing was working. And her savings were growing substantially since Josie had insisted, even after the adoption, that she continue to draw a "salary." After all, she used to give her "darling Bea" an allowance, even after college.

Although she had little sentiment about Christmas, each year Jade had dutifully put up the artificial tree and, with explicit directions from Josie that she now knew by heart, she placed each bulb and handmade item exactly where Josie wanted them. Thanks to Beaknose, all decorations that Jade had made as a very young girl had been thrown out when they moved to Rochester, but she found herself beginning to feel as attached to Josie's shiny globes and snowy angels as though it had been she and not Bea who had grown up with them.

As with most older people during holidays, Josie would start reminiscing, talking about Beatrice and what a perfect child she had been, all of which invariably caused Jade to reflect on the fact that no one would ever look back with pride or sentiment on *her* childhood.

After Mama left, the only thing Jade had liked about Christmas with Papa was the wonderful smell of pine trees, a rich, intoxicating scent that never came from Josie's plastic one. The need to tromp around in the woods would always be a part of who Jade was, for the pine scent and solitude was so much a part of what she had shared with Bear.

Outside, something caught Jade's attention as it fluttered past the window, like a white moth twirling in the wind, and she realized that it had started to snow. Later that afternoon, she went out to shovel the driveway and front walk, a perfect excuse to escape Josie's sentimental storytelling, and to exhilarate in the weather, as the fat, lazy flakes drifted with soft intention toward the place they were meant to land, while her breath turned to vapor.

Jade was tempted to lie down on her back on the snowy expanse, to fan her arms and legs with abandon and do what she hadn't done since Mama left—make a snow angel. She drew in her breath. *Was she really thinking about leaving a trace of herself?*

And the answer was a definite no, particularly when she found herself remembering the Christmas at the Roberts' house, the first *assignment* of her junior year at Rochester High. She had joined the family in the den where everyone had gathered to distribute the gifts piled beneath the tree, bright with ornaments and blinking lights. While everyone watched, Jade had been given the first gift—a red, oversized, acrylic sweater that smelled suspiciously of Goodwill. Right after that, before any other gifts were handed out, she was told, *not asked,* to start preparing what "Auntie Leslie" referred to as their traditional Christmas breakfast which, as it turned out, included making John Roberts' mother's coffeecake recipe, frying up two pounds of bacon, and putting together an egg, onion, mushroom, cheese, and tomato casserole.

"Don't forget what I taught you, *Jaydeen*: cook 'n clean, cook n' clean," "Auntie Leslie" had called gaily over her shoulder as she returned to enjoy the gift-opening with her family.

Jade smiled, recalling how she had fantasized using castor oil instead of olive oil in the casserole. Better than that, knowing "Auntie Leslie" was allergic to nuts, she had pictured rubbing the buttered coffee cake pan with peanuts before pouring in the batter. Well, at least she *had* wiped the dog's dish with each strip of bacon. As for her gift, she had stuffed the red sweater into a Goodwill bin in the Market Basket parking lot later that week.

They could take their Christmas and shove it.

Angels did not exist.

Over the years, Jade *never* did her shopping for Josie or herself in town. None of the local citizens ever saw her out and about; that went for whatever was needed— food, clothing, meds, or hiking through the woods. No one, and she meant NO ONE, was going to be able to put any of the pieces of Jade together.

Hell, she could hardly do that herself.

CHAPTER TWENTY-EIGHT

One day in early April, Jade drove over the Charles River to the Mount Auburn Cemetery in Cambridge, a favorite, quiet spot where she loved to walk. The day was bright and windy, with a film of stringy white clouds scuttling across the sky.

Along the path, her hair, caught up in a ponytail, bounced across her shoulder as she bent to observe crocuses and snowdrops that were nothing more than sharp green points lifting through the matted leaves. Pausing to watch a gray squirrel streak down a paper-white birch whose tender green buds slanted toward the sun, she suddenly pictured Bear so clearly that she almost expected him to step out from behind the mottled trunk of a maple, its bark slashed with old scars, just as he had so often materialized out of nowhere during those years of servitude to the *Bitches of Rochester*.

What had ever happened to him? It was a fleeting thought, but so poignant that she suddenly felt like weeping.

Barely fifteen minutes into her walk, Jade heard a call for help. Sprinting ahead, she followed the cries to where she found an older woman on the ground, clutching her leg. She was wearing what looked like designer jeans, a fake fur jacket, and a long cashmere scarf wrapped twice around her neck. She had already loosened the ties on her boots.

"Oh, thank goodness you heard me," she gasped as Jade bent over her. "I tripped on a tree root. I think it's my ankle."

Jade helped her to a standing position. "Since it's your right leg, you probably shouldn't drive," she told her.

"Then perhaps you'd be kind enough to call a cab for me," the woman said, her silvered brown hair falling loose from a soft bun at the nape of her neck.

"Well . . . where do you live?" Jade asked. Hesitating for a millisecond when the woman said Beacon Hill, she wondered about getting involved; but then, her training told her that she couldn't exactly walk away. "I'm a nurse. An LPN. I wouldn't mind driving you home," Jade told her.

Without a second thought, the woman agreed. "A nurse! That would be so kind of you. How lucky that you came along. I live on Pinckney Street, and don't worry about my car, I can just leave it where it is for now."

Jade found her way easily to the woman's address. There was a funny little bar called the Seventy-Seven Club that Jade had visited several times, and it was just around the corner from Pinckney. Miracle of miracles, she found a parking space almost in front of her building.

When the woman, who had introduced herself as Wendy Feinberg, invited her in for tea, Jade, curiously drawn to her, did not refuse.

"Am I glad you came along when you did," Wendy said, hopping cautiously over to a wing chair and allowing Jade to prop her leg on the footstool.

Glancing around the apartment, Jade saw that it was spacious and loaded with antiques, the windows and mirrors sparkling clean, the rugs understated and perfectly arranged.

"What's a lovely young woman like you doing walking alone," Wendy asked with a twinkle in her eye and the hint of a dimple on her right cheek, "and what's your name?"

"My name is Jade, and why's a woman like *you* walking alone?" Jade shot back, leaning down to take a look at the woman's ankle.

"Because I'm an independent woman," she retorted, "and if I want to do something, I do it. That's why," she said, quickly pushing Jade away. "And don't fuss with my foot; I'm sure it's nothing. Just a bruise or a slight sprain. Now, Jade, would you mind fixing us both a cup of tea? And don't be alarmed when you see a gun in the drawer."

"A gun?" Jade called back from the kitchen. "What in the world would you want that for in this secure apartment? I hope it's not loaded."

"For protection. And of course it's loaded," the woman answered. "I've had it ever since I lived in New York City years ago."

Jade put the kettle on the stove and found delicate bone china cups and saucers edged with gold in the cupboard, and sterling silverware in a drawer; and yes, there it was . . . a gun in the same drawer. How odd is that, she thought.

The tea was loose, imported, and smelled of an expensive specialty shop. Waiting for the water to boil, she went down a wide hallway, looking for the bathroom, and passed a bedroom with a graceful canopy bed draped in lace. She saw two antique dressers along the wall, and a vase of fresh cut flowers.

As a child, Jade had dreamed of sleeping in a bed like that, one that would make her feel like a princess. Suddenly, she was overcome with envy. The woman might have stumbled in the cemetery, but it was she, Jade, who had stumbled into this place of privilege.

Jade sat on a loveseat upholstered in royal blue crushed velvet while they sipped tea and ate delicious lemon cookies she had found in the pantry. Running her hand across the elegant fabric, she noticed that the window facing the street held matching velvet drapes. It was late afternoon, the sunlight striped across the gleaming hardwood floor, and the muffled sounds of the street drifted into the room. This was class, she told herself—all the way.

They exchanged the usual bits and pieces of information, with Jade taking pains not to say too much, and even though she did confess to having been an orphan, once she had said it, she felt a pang of disloyalty to Josie. And she did talk a bit about her nursing career.

"I think things happen for a reason," Wendy said, after she revealed the fact that she was alone in the world, "don't you? I mean, we were destined to meet."

"Why is that?" Jade replied. Let her be the one to push us forward, Jade thought, her mind already racing ahead, planning how she could fit Wendy into her weekly schedule. Josie, who by now trusted her explicitly, had long ago given up asking what she did when she took time away from the house.

Wendy brought her teacup to her lips, smiling at Jade over the rim. "Because I recently arrived from New York, and you're the first friendly person I've met since I got here."

So it was arranged, with surprisingly little exchange of information, that Jade would "stop by" for tea on

Sunday afternoons, a day that she and Josie had agreed long ago that she needed for herself. Experiencing an unexpected feeling of buoyancy, Jade sensed that something was going to change. There was some quality about Wendy that appealed to her. Was it the woman's sense of independence? Her positive attitude? Whatever it was, she was ready to stretch herself, to open herself to friendship.

Unlike Josie, Wendy wasn't mourning a lost child, because she'd never had children. Perhaps as a consequence, their conversations were more intellectual, thanks to her apparent total immersion in culture which included support of the American Repertory Company in Cambridge and frequent trips to the Museum of Fine Arts.

"I have season tickets to the symphony," Wendy said, and then, as she went on to talk about Beethoven and Brahms and guest conductors, Jade figured out that B.S.O. meant Boston Symphony Orchestra.

"You must come with me to see the Degas," Wendy announced, sounding almost imperious.

Jade searched her memory from high school art class. "He was the one who painted the ballerinas, right?"

"He did love those ladies of the stage," Wendy said. "But remember, he needed models. The human form. And the dancers were there anyway, practicing, happy to model for next to nothing." She threw back her head as if imitating Degas' long-necked figures.

Jade nodded and sipped her tea as delicately as she knew how while she tried to take in this world of culture that Wendy took for granted. It was a world to which Jade had never dreamed she would be given access, and the thought of extending the narrow boundaries of the life she had created with Josie made her head spin.

After their first meeting, Wendy never pressed for family history again. "I'm just so grateful to have met you," she told Jade a few weeks later as they drove to the theater in Cambridge that Jade had learned to call the ART, to see *A Streetcar Named Desire*, a play that Wendy said was a classic that might resonate with Jade.

"I don't give a hang what happened to you before now," she had said, "but you can't say you are an orphan anymore, because we are *family* in the best sense of the word."

Plays, concerts, museums, lectures—activities planned and paid for by Wendy, who was opening a door into Jade's own possibilities, into what she believed she could become. When Wendy noticed Jade looking at her shelves loaded with books, she told her to take one home with her. Wendy approved of Jade's choice: *The Plays of Tennessee Williams.*

"As you read each play, we could discuss it," she suggested. "I'd enjoy that."

No one had ever offered to discuss a book with her before. It made Jade feel smart and sophisticated.

Only once more did Wendy ask about her childhood, and did not seem offended when Jade told her that her past was a closed book.

"I'm just thinking that it's not good to live so much inside yourself, Jade. It's an exile, actually. It makes you different."

"I don't mind being different. Actually, I like it."

And although she would have died rather than admit it, Jade knew that she did not want to be different, at least not in the way Wendy intended it. This was a world she wanted to be part of—a far cry from Rochester— one that would reject all that that narrow-minded community represented. If she could only tell Wendy.

But that was impossible. Instead, she would spread her wings, at least as far as being dependent on Josie would allow her.

Would it always be true, she found herself wondering, that her life should be constricted by the demands of others?

CHAPTER TWENTY-NINE

Josie's husband had been a high school English teacher who, over the years, had accumulated an amazing collection of books, now lining the shelves of the study which had become Jade's office shortly after she'd moved in. Josie acted pleased when Jade, spurred on by Wendy's encouragement to expand her mind, began perusing her husband's library. And somehow it came as no surprise to Jade to find how much she enjoyed reading, especially now that she could discuss the books with Wendy. *She would've done better in school if shit hadn't happened in her life, like, being bounced around between the "Aunties" all through high school.*

She treasured the quiet, comforting smell of leather softened with age, the patina of the cherry wood desk, and the not quite musty smell of each book that Josie's husband had carefully arranged alphabetically by author. Adams, Bronte, Browning, all the way to Wordsworth and Yeats. It was her favorite place where, in a weird way, she felt a sense of security and approval from Mr. Gerard, someone she had never met. "Dad," she said out loud with a tentative smile, trying out the sound of the word, yet knowing full well that she sure as hell had never gotten anything that even closely resembled approval from her own father. As a child, Jade had thought of herself, at the most, as being dull and plain, just as she was certain others had seen her. Except, of course, for Bear, who had said that her eyes were the shade of a particular green stone found in ancient Indian burial grounds that, when mellowed over time, looked like jade. Even so, she hadn't taken it as a compliment, but rather a simple statement of fact. *But she had never forgotten how his words had made her feel.*

For years, Jade had made a point of going out Thursday evenings, when she'd get dressed up, actually pleased with how she looked, and then take the T or drive into Boston to eat somewhere special or go to a movie or simply roam around. Josie accepted her pattern of comings and goings, and like numerous other aspects of their relationship, she did not question Jade.

In Boston, she'd fall in step with people rushing in all directions, or couples strolling together, buying pretzels or hotdogs or ice cream from peddlers' carts stationed on almost every corner. Summer was Jade's favorite time, when the hot August air that draped itself over the city rose in ripples above the cement and children in swimsuits danced around fire hydrants, their spray nozzles fanning a cascade of water into the streets. She especially enjoyed wandering through the Public Garden, sipping the latte that she often carried with her as she toured the neatly manicured gardens, admiring the brilliant colors of the daylilies and the murmuring pigeons, their wings rippling in the light.

Part of the charm and mystery of the city for her was to browse bookstores that were open until midnight and pause at a street corner to listen to a tenor saxophonist play a soulful rendition of *Birth of the Blues*, as fat mellow notes floated out, soaring upward in the balmy air.

Once, when she was twelve, Jade had gone to Boston with Beaknose and Angie to ride on the swan boats and Angie had thrown up on Jade's lap. It was a disgusting puddle of pineapple they'd had for breakfast, and Jade could still picture how she had reacted by shoving Angie away from her and screaming at the top of her voice, "Stop the car!" Beaknose had made her wait until she found a place to park, and then had told her that if she ever raised a hand to her daughter again, she would be severely punished. Remembering the incident now, Jade could no longer ignite her old hatred of her stepmother. Since living with Josie, she had taken many trips on the swan boats, watching groups of children laughing, leaning into their mothers, having fun.

When Josie asked Jade what she did Thursday nights, she told her she liked to attend book readings and signings at favorite bookstores, and Josie had said how proud she was that "her girl" was continuing her education. "Just like my Bea," she repeated, "always trying to better herself."

The constant comparisons had long since begun to rattle Jade's nerves. *Why couldn't she be just like herself?* Nobody, until Wendy, had ever really looked at her as a unique person with the potential to really *be* someone. Maybe Mama hadn't seen her that way either. Perhaps that was why she left.

With Beaknose, Jade had been a thing to be tolerated, part of the package deal. And with the *assignments*, she had learned to be what they expected her to be with no life of her own.

Finally, she knew why her life had been so miserable. It was because she had not been in a position to call the shots. And you could bet your ass, she was now. No soul was ever going to tell her what to do. Never again in her life.

Those Thursday evenings, when she delighted in exploring downtown Boston, Jade would stop occasionally for a drink, choosing a popular after-theater bar or one of the many high-class hotel lounges, like the Four Seasons, where she often met older, wealthy men, unattached for the evening. It amazed her how easily she could talk about politics or books or scientific research without a sense of inferiority. On the contrary, she'd slip effortlessly into the role of a vivacious, disarming woman who responded to the laments of those men as the only person at that moment who understood them. Almost like a split personality, Jade could feel herself transform. That's when she had learned how simple it was to indulge in casual sex. But never for love.

Where this outgoing veneer came from, she didn't have a clue. Maybe out of a deeply entrenched sadness, but for sure, she knew it was superficial—no depth or true emotion—but those men were so self-involved, it didn't matter. Unknowingly, they fell into her spider's web where she could remain unhurt and in charge. *She was always the one who left them.*

Perhaps that's how Beaknose had snared Papa— when he must have been thinking about himself, instead of his daughter who had needs certainly as great as his.

With each of these casual encounters, Jade was hardly aware of how her aloneness deepened into a hole through which darkness poured like liquid tar, sealing her off from her anger, her enormous grief. But she didn't care because she wasn't looking for a meaningful relationship. It had not been planned, that first time, a one-night stand. But the third and fourth . . .? She was just having some fun. No commitment, no talk of love or future. She didn't have these rendezvous for money; it was for the sense of power and control, although one man did offer to pay her, which, of course, she refused and laughed about on the way home. Just a little flirtation at a bar, not much more than an hour in a hotel room, and back home early enough not to worry Josie. As usual, she had to think about someone else besides herself.

And then it happened. Wendy announced that she was going to spend a few weeks in the Caribbean with an old friend from New York. Yes, she had asked Jade, *at the last minute*, if she would like to join them, knowing full well that it would be impossible because of her work. *Because of Josie.* It was hard for Jade to fathom why she felt so hurt and abandoned.

The first Thursday after that, Jade decided to drive into Boston, hoping to push back the poisonous waves of jealousy she felt every time she thought about Wendy and her friend in the Islands. Wendy, having fun— without her.

The bar at the Biltmore was not overly crowded and it didn't take long for a man to start up a conversation. She certainly had no way of predicting that things would get way out of control when she agreed to meet him, someone she only knew as Joe, in his room on the ninth floor. He told her to allow about ten minutes after he left the bar.

When he greeted her in his room, he had a fresh drink in hand. "Take your clothes off," he said without ceremony, after locking the door.

So much for foreplay, she thought. "Let's slow down here a minute," she said. "How about a drink for me?"

"I already bought you one at the bar," he told her, unzipping his fly. "Take your clothes off," he said again, louder than before.

"What happened to the charming man I met just an hour ago?" she retorted. She had never been treated like a whore before, and she didn't like it. Perhaps she should have guessed that something like this might happened when he had suggested that she not accompany him upstairs.

But when she started to leave, her dignity preserved, he grabbed her purse. "Let's see who you *really* are, Miss High and Mighty."

"Give me that, you bastard!" she cried, lunging for it.

This was when he slapped her hard across the face.

Her rage met his—quick and furious. Instinctively, Jade snatched a bronze-based lamp from a table next to her, and, with all her might, crashed it against his head.

Without a sound, he crumbled to the floor.

An icy calm descended on her as she stepped over him, picked up her purse, and started for the door, and then, on impulse, she grabbed his wallet that was sitting on the dresser.

Unobserved, she slipped through the lobby and just walked away.

As she drove home, silent bolts of heat lightning pulsed through the darkness and shimmered like wild silk across the night sky. Her hands trembled on the steering wheel. *What the hell had just happened?* One thing was clear. Her sex-for-fun days were over. Drifting into a freefall of indifference, she refused to consider that there could be consequences for what she had done. She thought about the family photos he'd shown her when they were still at the bar: big smiles, straight white teeth, a blond-haired daughter wearing a skimpy cheerleading outfit, a gawky son with a basketball under his arm. Someone with a family like that would not want to report an incident in a hotel room with a young woman. He'd think up some story. She was certain of that.

Any regrets about her attack migrated to her subconscious, simmering there with an undercurrent of violence; what was most important was that she had maintained control of the situation—didn't lose her head. She hoped he'd learned a lesson. She sure as hell had.

CHAPTER THIRTY

The call came through at ten when Bear and Lappas were coming out of Dunkin' with their coffee and donuts. "You guys better get over to the Biltmore. It sounds like a homicide," Yvonne Garneau's voice rang out from their car, loud and confident. Bear looked up at a flag that snapped against the pole planted on a concrete circle in the parking lot. A slow drizzle was threatening to turn to rain. A murder. Just what they needed on a day like this. Jumping into their car, they headed over to Copley Square, where police cars and emergency vehicles were parked three-deep in the street and uniformed officers were crowded about the front entrance. The doorman looked extremely perturbed, having to calm the guests as he guided them out of the building.

Upstairs, on the ninth floor, Bear flashed his badge at the officer standing at the door, and then led the way across the room. There was a blur of activity as forensic techs and police officers attended to preserving the crime scene, meticulously looking for every possible clue of value, making sure that nothing was disturbed.

"Are you the manager?" Bear asked a man in a suit who was standing in the middle of the room, wringing his hands.

"Yes. Oh my God, this is awful. We've never had a murder in this hotel. Not on *my* watch," he added emphatically.

"I am Homicide Detective Kuruk and this is Detective Lappas. What can you tell us about the victim?" Bear asked him. He was all too well-acquainted with civilian hysteria in the face of raw violence such as this, which had left its naked victim sprawled across the floor.

"Jacob Henderson from Wisconsin. Just checked in yesterday. Comes to Boston every month or so." He was staring at the carpet as he spoke; Bear figured he was worried about getting rid of the bloodstains.

"Was he traveling alone?"

"Yes. Always. But . . ."

"But what?"

"Well, he has been observed to have company in his room on several occasions. Look, I don't want to get the man in trouble."

Lappas laughed. "I guess he's had about all the trouble he's ever going to get."

Bear glared at his partner, and then returned his attention to the manager. "Who found the body?"

"The maid. She went in to clean the room. And don't worry, she didn't touch a thing. She reported straight to me and I didn't enter this room until the police arrived."

"Please get me his registration card and any other information you may have on him," Bear said, dismissing him before turning to the officer that seemed to be in charge.

"He had several hundred bucks in his pocket," the officer told them, "and a top-of-the-line Rolex, so it doesn't look like robbery, but we can't find a wallet. Couldn't make an ID until we talked to the manager."

There's a certain miasma of violence at the scene of every crime, Bear thought, as he looked down at the man, vulnerable in his nakedness—it lingers, like a choking residue, a grim, almost tangible reminder that some unspeakable evil has taken place. Crouching down, Bear looked closely at the victim. *What the hell had gone on in this room?*

The medical examiner stood, ripped off his gloves, and signaled that he was finished; the body could be taken to the morgue. The victim, it seemed, had died of a massive brain hemorrhage, which had probably been caused by his having been struck by the heavy table lamp that was lying on the floor next to his body.

"There is no sign of sexual activity and no apparent struggle. Looks like he wasn't expecting what he got. Whoever hit him with that lamp had a powerful wallop— probably in a moment of crazed anger."

It was likely, Bear thought, after looking over the forensic report, that this was going to be another one of those unsolved crimes, so prevalent in Boston lately—especially those involving out-of-town people. Nothing but blurred fingerprints, which was to be expected in a hotel room; no apparent motive, no trail to follow. Two long strands of dark brown hair had been recovered, probably from the last occupant of the room. And that was it. Nothing else. Another random crime, the worst kind to try to solve. There is no system to soothe the unfairness of things, he thought, justice was without scope. It might snag the stealer of a car, yet great invasive crimes like this one would be dismissed— crimes that took place between two people without a witness. The guilty seldom paid. There was no religion, no government, that could relieve that kind of injustice.

CHAPTER THIRTY-ONE

Darkness pressed at the windows like a bad dream, closing in on Jade while she sat with the *Boston Globe* spread out before her on Josie's kitchen table, her eyes transfixed on the news item. *What the hell? That was the night before last. He wasn't dead when I left—he couldn't have been.* Her lips moved wordlessly as she read the story carefully, sat back, and finally laid her head on the table. Why did these things happen to her?

Hearing the muted sound of a neighbor running a leaf blower, she found herself remembering, incongruously, that she needed to prepare Josie's yard for winter. Although it was only 7:40 on the kitchen clock, it felt much later. The day had lost its shape, distorted under the weight of the unexpected.

Mechanically, Jade began making breakfast for Josie. Breaking eggs into a bowl, she tried not to think of how devastated Josie would be if this came out. Not to even consider how it would ruin her own life. The last thing in the world she wanted to do was hurt Josie or give her reason to feel ashamed, even though she had had no choice. She'd had to protect herself. Suddenly, turning off the flame under the scrambled eggs, Jade reached for her purse that she always hung carelessly over the back of a chair. Plunging her hand into it, she pulled out the man's wallet and spread the contents out on the counter.

With scissors, she methodically cut each credit card, his driver's license, social security card, photos of his lovely family, and finally the wallet itself, into pieces not much larger than a postage stamp. As she worked, it started to rain, steadily now, water running across the roof in rivulets to drip rhythmically onto the window's ledge. Scooping all the little cuttings into a bowl, Jade spent fifteen minutes in the first floor powder room, flushing all evidence of Jacob Henderson down the toilet.

He had been a vicious man, she told herself while buttering toast. God only knew what he might have done to her if she hadn't acted so quickly. It could have been *her* lying on that floor. She had been so frightened. He could have killed her. No one could blame her for defending herself. He didn't get anything that wasn't coming to him, yet, it had not been her intent to kill him—just to shut up his ugly face and get the hell out of there. No one could blame her, even though she had now managed to kill *two* men. But after all, both times it had been self-defense. Anyone in her place would have done the same. Surely there were other women like her in the world. Just think of all the unsolved crimes. *And yet, and yet . . . what if she had been identified? And then prosecuted?* The confluence of these events, these *murders,* made Jade test the fault lines of her life for glimpses of the kind of insanity that led her to kill—twice. What, in the end, was the limit of what she was capable of doing?

Feeling a pain travel from her stomach up through her throat, Jade had to keep swallowing, pushing against a steady burn of regret, beyond which lurked her own culpability. She only knew that she was capable of acting quickly when threatened or rejected and that she rarely stopped to consider consequences. She'd had to do that her whole life, except for when Bear had stood up for her, and look where *that* had got him.

But, this had to be the end of Jadine Tomecelli and all her bad luck when, in those sad old days, Bear had been the only good thing that had happened to her. Now, as Jade Gerard, her life could be different. It already was. There was Josie. And Wendy.

Yes, that was how she had to think of it. Jadine had killed those men to save her own life. From now on, from this very moment, Jade would think of others before herself.

CHAPTER THIRTY-TWO

Over the past year, Jade had noticed that Josie's age had finally caught up with her. She looked shrunken and vulnerable. What little additional flesh she had carried had disappeared months ago, and now her muscles had also vanished, leaving her shoulder bones sticking up like knobs. Her cheeks had sunken in as well, so that her face was merely a skull with a thin sheet of skin over it. It saddened her to see her "mother" diminished. She couldn't imagine the future without Josie.

When had she begun to stay in bed all the time, looking so shriveled and frail?

The house had taken on a medicinal smell much like that of Serene when she had first worked there as an aide cleaning bathrooms with bleach when the patients had near misses. Cheryl had warned her to just keep breathing normally until her senses went dead, but now those same disinfectant smells seemed to cling to the inside of her nose, even when she was away from the house.

Josie had started repeating those annoying stories of Beatrice as a child, Beatrice as a perfect teenager, Beatrice in college, always the attentive and loving daughter, bringing forth all those memories as though to look at each, fold it carefully, and preserve it in some cedar-lined chest, not unlike Jade's retreat box. But she was becoming weary of grieving Josie's grief, and making allowances for her seventy-nine years. It seemed as though Josie had lost interest in Jade—*after everything she had done for her*—nursed her, cleaned her house, painted it, thrown out junk; cared for the place as though it were her own. And the yard was absolutely lovely, the best groomed in the entire neighborhood, with a thriving purple smoke tree that Josie had helped her plant that first summer right in the center of the back yard.

Josie's mind was definitely slipping, all except for one lucid thread of inquiry that she had recently latched onto, with tenacity; a subject that had been taboo between them for so long—Jade's real mother.

"So, tell me about your parents," she would say over and over again. "What was your dear mother like?"

"I told you a million times, Josephine. I was an orphan until I met you."

"Why are you mad at me—that's what you do when you're mad—you call me Josephine."

At times like these, Jade became so impatient with the old woman, it was difficult not to wonder if she had made a bad bargain in staying with her. But she had needed a mother, even one who loved her own child more than she could ever love her.

"I don't want to talk about it," she would say.

"But your mother must have loved you so," Josie would protest.

"I never knew her."

"Did she die young?"

"Okay. Yes. She died young."

"Tell me about her, please Jadie. Was she as pretty as my Bea?"

"Go to sleep." *Be quiet and go to sleep, Josie.* Day after day the now-pathetic old woman kept badgering Jade about her mother, forgetting that, right from the very beginning, that subject had been forbidden, and refusing now, in her growing senility, to listen to Jade when she reminded her of it.

"You can tell me, Jade," she'd whine. "I won't repeat it to a soul."

She didn't even know how dangerous truth could be, Jade thought. All the tiny shattering seeds it carried. Besides, her only remaining memories of her mother only gave her pain.

"Tell me, tell me, tell me about your mama," was, it seemed, a constant refrain now.

Josie was slipping away, losing her mind to cobwebs, trapped in forgetfulness and confusion, and then suddenly, repeatedly, she'd look up at Jade with her watery blue eyes. "I don't want you any more," she'd say in a quarrelsome voice, "I want my Bea. Go tell her you're being mean to me. I want Bea to make you go away." Jade's sympathy turned to hurt. She had become so sick of hearing the dead girl's name.

"Shh, shh, go to sleep," she said now, forcing two sleeping pills down Josie's throat and then sitting back, watching her until she drifted off.

What should I do? She asked herself over and over again. Josie would be horrified to see herself like this.

"Help! She's trying to kill me," Josie called out in a faint breath a few weeks later, closing her eyes, and clutching at Jade's arm. Brushing her hand away, Jade tucked the old woman in so tightly she could not move.

Months of this, all through the darkest, most paralyzing winter she could remember, until Jade wanted to scream as Josie became increasingly impossible to care for. Every time Jade raised a spoon to those withered lips, Josie would clamp her mouth shut or spit the food out onto the bed covers or down the front of whatever Jade was wearing.

Laying her head on Josie's bony chest, Jade cried softly. "You've got to stop this Josie, I can't take it anymore. Please be like your old self."

"I hate you. You killed my precious Bea. You've taken everything from me."

The petals of flowers, mostly daisies, caught Jade's eye as they dropped onto the bureau across the room . . . the bouquet she had put there to give cheer to the room.

"Someone. I need someone to help me," was Josie's constant cry now.

And that touched Jade at a level that even she could not understand except that she had loved this woman once, and her love had, gradually, since this terrible thing had happened to Josie's mind, turned to disgust and pity—a lethal combination.

✻ ✻ ✻

It finally happened on a beautiful spring day, a day seemingly no different from any other, when Jade folded back Josie's patchwork quilt to find that her nightgown had slipped off her shoulders and twisted up around her thighs, exposing her nipples like little wizened currants. She was so thin now that, beneath her ribs, Jade could see the faint pulsing of her heart.

Leaning over her, Jade stared into her vacant eyes, trying to see some sign of recognition, but the Josie she had once known and grown to love had disappeared months before. Her Josie was no longer there, and what remained wanted some sort of deliverance which she—and only she—could deliver.

Finally, finally, without giving herself time to think further, she filled her lungs with the fetid air of the sickroom and lowered her mouth over Josie's. At the same time, she gently closed her nose. It seemed like no more than seconds before it was over.

Sliding off the bed, Jade went into the bathroom for a washcloth. She knew her saliva needed to be washed from around Josie's mouth, although if any question came up about it, she'd just say that she had tried mouth-to-mouth resuscitation. Then she returned to Josie's bedroom, gently closing her eyes and smoothing her disheveled hair close around her ashen face, a face that had once been so precious.

She gave me no choice, saying those horrible things to me. I loved her. Why wasn't that enough? I told her that I was an orphan. Why wouldn't she listen to me, damn it? Now she's ruined everything, and I am alone again.

As Jade picked up the phone to dial 911, she looked at the corner whatnot with Josie's prized collection of blue delft—a miniature kerosene lamp, a creamer in the shape of a cow, a Dutch boy and girl figurine, little plates with windmills— all the things that spoke of the beauty Josie had once cherished. This was where she had grown comfortable with a sense of belonging as Josie's daughter. Because she *was* that. There was no one else. No husband, no children, no siblings, or cousins. Not even close friends. She and Josie had lived only for one another, and it had been enough. More than enough, for a long time.

As she waited for the ambulance, her hand resting on her retreat box which she hadn't felt the need to even look at in years, Jade stared at the crown molding, the thought crossing her mind that it needed painting. Josie only weighed eighty pounds. How much longer would she have lasted? This was nothing like the filthy landlord in the shower, or the man in the Biltmore Hotel. Those had been acts of self-defense. With Josie, it was an act of love and mercy.

Jade didn't feel guilty, just incredibly sad. She knew that she had saved Josie from a drawn-out, agonizing death, and, thank God, long before dementia set in, she had told Josie that she had grown to love her like a mother. At least there was that.

But in the end, a difficult truth struggled to the surface. Josie had demanded too much of her. Eventually, everyone demanded too much.

CHAPTER THIRTY-THREE

So it was official. Josephine Gerard had died of natural causes and left *everything* to her daughter, Jade Gerard. The house, the car, her investments—everything—even her wedding ring, which the medical examiner had removed from Josie's finger. Jade decided to wrap the gold ring in a glove from Josie's drawer and put it in her retreat box. Somehow it didn't seem right to wear it with Josie's name and wedding date engraved inside the band.

Everyone was so solicitous, especially the local cops. Even a couple of neighbors, whom Jade had avoided through the years, tried to deliver casseroles, which she refused. "Vegan," she gave as a reason even though it wasn't true. It was kind of them to offer their condolences, but she didn't want people prying into her life. When, eventually, they left her alone, she was grateful and relieved.

Jade didn't mind waiting in her ultimate retreat—within the walls of Josie's house which was now hers and hers alone, where she felt safe, grateful to be held in this sling of time as she struggled with something churning inside her. Not guilt, surely. She had done Josie a kindness, released her from further suffering. And released herself as well. The thought stunned her, because, if *that* had been the case, then one could say that she had *used* Josie, and she could swear to God that she had not. She was aware of certain truths, but could not bear to know what she knew. Hadn't she actually grown to *love* Josie; taken care of her for almost six years? That alone was certainly proof enough that her motives had been selfless. Josie would not have wanted to linger in that terrible fog of dementia. She had said so, many times.

Sadness loomed from the shadows of the room like a faceless creature with a dark cape. Jade yearned for Wendy, who had gone on another trip, this time to Tuscany to stay with an old, dear friend who had bought and renovated a 19th century villa. And because, as she said, Jade was preoccupied with a dying client, now was as good a time as any to go. Reluctantly, Jade had urged her friend to take the trip, and have a wonderful time. But she had lied. She was used to Wendy being accessible and resented the fact that she obviously didn't care whether or not Jade might need her more than ever at a time like this.

Down in the basement, the oil-fired furnace clicked on, rumbling indifferently. Slowly, as if each foot weighed a ton, Jade picked up Josie's afghan, the one she had crocheted so many years ago when her fingers were nimble, and climbed the stairs to Josie's bedroom. For a moment, she just sat on the bed staring at the wall, trying to figure out what to do next. Well, actually she knew what to do—she would spend more time with Wendy upon her return, and, fearful of having too much time on her hands, she would find another client.

Josie had provided her with something that she had desperately needed, at least at first. And now that need had returned with a vengeance.

But her mind was in turmoil. Right now, all that she needed was sleep—a long, deep sleep, without dreams.

CHAPTER THIRTY-FOUR

As the weeks passed, Jade was surprised to see how easily she was adjusting to Josie's absence. Everything in the house took on a different meaning, now that they belonged to her, and she cleaned and dusted Josie's belongings, each one with a memory that she had passed on to Jade. Now those memories became Jade's as she handled them lovingly.

Being a woman who lived by routine, six weeks after Josie's death, Jade stepped into her closet this Thursday afternoon and chose a soft, apple-green cashmere sweater-set to compliment her black Versace skirt, an outfit Josie had given her last year for an evening in Boston.

One last check in the mirror, and Jade was satisfied that her look was as classy as old money. Taking a sixteen-inch strand of matched pearls from Josie's jewelry box, she remembered Josie had marveled once, that with a name like Tomecelli, how could she have ended up looking like a green-eyed Irish beauty with her dark hair and fair skin? *Josie had always said such nice things and been so generous . . .*

She was grateful. She truly was—would always be.

Once in town, Jade decided to eat at the Copley Plaza before going to a movie. Seeing a line in front of the dining room, she checked her watch.

"It's because there's a convention," a woman in front of her commented as Jade turned to leave. She was slightly stooped and Jade could see the gentle curve of her back beneath her jacket.

Why was she attracted to older women, she wondered? Josie had replaced Mama, and if she had to choose right now between the two, it would be Josie, in a heartbeat. It was rather a surprising thought . . . that she had finally and completely let her mother go.

The woman suggested that, if she was alone, they might share a table, and when Jade agreed, she signaled to the maître d', changing her reservation to a table for two. The woman began to speak as soon as they were seated.

"I live here, on the seventh floor—my own suite," she told Jade as soon as they were sitting opposite one another. "I'm here on the proviso that I take care of myself. If not, they'll make me leave. That was the deal. I had to remain completely independent." The woman's sparse brows creased with worry as she spoke in a confidential whisper, her voice rushing at Jade across the table.

"Nothing could be that bad," Jade said soothingly, patting her liver-spotted hand. "There's always a solution. Now, my name is Jade Gerard. And you are . . .?"

"Of course. Where are my manners? I am Sophia Markeha," she said, reaching out in greeting. "Living at this hotel was the best solution for me—maid service, dining room—I'm eighty-nine and have buried every last relative. All my friends are gone, too. But I'm still here, more's the pity."

Jade waited. *Could it be happening again? And so soon?*

"The least I could do is treat you to a fabulous dinner," Sophia said, handing her a menu. "The sky's the limit— choose anything you'd like. The filet is fabulous."

To watch her sitting regally in her chair, you'd never guess that she had just seemed so frightened, Jade thought, as she ordered a modestly-priced meal.

I don't want to take advantage of this lady.

The following Tuesday, after they had met for lunch again, Jade stood at Sophia's window on the seventh floor of the Plaza. The slender mirrored face of the John Hancock building rising fifty stories on the southern edge of Copley Square reflected the big brownstone Trinity Church back upon itself. Opposite the church was the Boston Public Library. The early spring sun pierced the window in a fine, thin tube of light.

By the desk, Sophia was rummaging about frantically. "What I want to know is what you think about this letter from the manager," she said at last, waving a piece of hotel stationery under Jade's nose, her face sallow except for a rosy blotch of rouge on each cheek. "Can they really make me leave? Even though I have never been delinquent in paying my bill?" Her fear of being forced out seemed to buzz around her like a force field.

"But you told me that someone complained to the manager when you kept trying your key in their lock."

"That was only because I got off on the wrong floor."

"Didn't he say it wasn't the first time?"

"I suppose that my memory has slipped a bit," Sophia admitted, "but I *did* pay the bill. I'm sure of it."

"I think that's true of all of us," Jade said, partly to be polite, and partly because she imagined that there were events in her own life that she remembered incorrectly—moments that, for her own mental health, she needed to forget. Or, at the very least, revise. *Everyone did that, didn't they?*

"I've made my way alone for so long now—outlived everybody," Sophia said, tears running down her cheeks.

Jade put her arm around the woman's bent shoulder, and drew her close, a gesture completely foreign to her, and wondered if she should get involved. Maybe this was the same kind of divine intervention that Josie had referred to when she spoke of how they had met at Serene. There is a kind of fate to the universe and a certain randomness, regardless of what you do or don't do. In helping others, Jadine was pleasing herself. It was a way of insinuating herself into people's lives, feeding off their needs and their loneliness. The sadness she felt for strangers, for the entire world, did not feel selfish so much as a kind of elevated consciousness, a heightened sensitivity to the truth.

"I've been thinking," Jade said. "Perhaps you'd like to come live with me for a while. I—I know something about how difficult it can feel to be alone, and I have a pleasant house in Brookline. We could be company for one another," she added with a smile.

"Would you? I mean, could I?" Sophia cried. "You'd do that for some old lady you just met?" Such gratitude made Jade squirm. The neediness in this woman's voice, so reminiscent of Josie.

"You know, there was something about you, Jade," she went on. "I sensed it the moment we met, and it would be amazingly simple because before I moved into the hotel, I sold everything. Nothing here belongs to me except for my clothes and a few things in that chest of drawers. I converted everything to cash when I sold my home three years ago, you see. It's all in the hotel safe. I don't trust stocks and bonds and such. Cash and carry. That's my motto." She gave a wily chuckle that sounded like a bark.

Partly to put her at ease and give her time to think about her offer, Jade recited a brief sketch of her recent past for Sophia: Serene, going to school to become an LPN, and then the years she had lived with Josie.

"So you see," Jade concluded, with what she hoped was a reassuring smile, "caring for elderly ladies is not exactly new for me."

"I'm willing if you are. I can't get over your generosity, though. Why me?"

"Why *not* you? Perhaps it's meant to be. Maybe it's something I need at least as much as you do. I've been lonely without Josie."

And it was true. Of course there had been a certain freedom in her life lately. She could hardly wait to see Wendy again and be part of her scene. But something deeper was calling out to her now. Sophia needed her. No, they needed one another. And, she told herself, let come of it what will.

At ten sharp, Jade met Sophia and a porter standing by her bags in the lobby of the Copley Plaza, and without saying much more than hello, she guided them out the door, said something to the uniformed doorman, then walked away. He stood between the gilded lions and whistled piercingly for a cab.

"That woman said that you are leaving us for good, Mrs. Markeha. Is that true?"

"Yes, I'm afraid it is. It's time for me to move on."

"She told me to have the cab take you and your luggage to The Lowell Tea Room," he said as he gestured at Jade's retreating back.

"Thank you for everything, Joseph."

"We'll miss you, ma'am," he told Sophia, once she was settled in the taxicab.

While waiting two doors down from the Tea Room, Jade listened to the birds right above her, pouring their hearts out in trees just beginning to bud. After the cabby arrived, leaving Sophia on the sidewalk with her few belongings, Jade stepped forward and picked up her suitcase. "My car is this way, you just hold tight to my arm."

They had put everything on the back seat of Jade's Nissan except for an oversized zippered bag which Sophia placed firmly on her lap, both hands folded through the handles. If she had been confused as to why Jade hadn't just met her at the hotel, she never said a word.

It had probably been an unnecessary decision, Jade thought now, all that subterfuge. But even though it may defy logic, it was almost impossible to change her old, entrenched fear of detection, of exposure, of being *known*.

CHAPTER THIRTY-FIVE

Sophia was a lot more fragile than she'd first appeared. As soon as they came into the house, Jade realized that she would have to make a spot for her on the first floor. After clearing out the little sewing room off the kitchen, she dragged the single bed from Bea's room down the stairs, set it up, and made the bed with fresh sheets. While Sophia waited in the living room, comfortable in Josie's old chair, still with the zippered bag on her lap, she watched as Jade brought the bureau down the stairs, one drawer at a time.

"You shouldn't be lifting those heavy things," Sophia called after her.

"Oh, don't worry about me. I'm stronger than I look."

"I am so grateful," Sophia said softly. "It must have been providence for us to be there, at the dining room, at exactly the same time."

"I'm glad, too, that I was there," Jade said as she struggled the rest of the bureau into the sewing room.

"It's so nice to be taken care of," the old woman told her. "You're an angel."

Jade laughed. "Well, I don't know about that."

✢ ✢ ✢

After breakfast the next morning, they were sitting at the kitchen table with a second cup of tea. Already, the first birds were beginning with single notes, hesitantly, as if their instinct for the light might be mistaken. The sun had just broken through the lower branches of the lindens that grew in front of the house.

"I need to talk with you about something," Sophia told her. "I want to pay you for allowing me to be here, in your lovely home; this incredible gift you are offering me. Would one thousand dollars a week be enough?" When Jade did not respond immediately, she said, "or more . . . double that. There's plenty of money, it's all in that black bag—over two hundred thousand—take it all. I can't put a value on what you have offered me." She was leaning forward, clutching the arms of the chair.

"Stop, Sophia. I didn't bring you here for your money. I am an orphan. It seems as if I am always looking for a mother. In the oddest places," Jade added, smiling tentatively, keenly aware of how true that was. With Josie's death, she had had that old feeling of desertion, of abandonment—an emptiness that only a mother could fill.

Sophia reached toward her, and Jade took her hand, the bones were as weightless as spun glass. "Your home is like a . . . like . . ." Her voice broke, tears rimmed her eyes.

"Like a retreat?" Jade said.

"Oh, yes, like the most heavenly retreat. All my fears are put to rest now that I'm here with you."

Embarrassed, Jade stood to clear the table. Sophia gave off a faint scent of lilac, and to her dismay, Jade didn't mind it. Actually, it was lovely. *Could she have outgrown that association with Mama?* Maybe, at last, she would plant a lilac bush, just outside the back steps, where its fragrance could come in through any open window.

"Wait," Sophia said, "please sit a moment longer, there's something else I need you to know." Leaning her head back against the wall next to the table, she closed her eyes. "I should have told you before I accepted your invitation. It's true that I have no one to take care of me. But I'm going to need more care than I told you about. You see, Jade dear, I don't have long to live. Maybe a year, probably less. It's uterine cancer and as a nurse, you must know what that means. How unfair is that? I had three miscarriages and no children."

Jade stared at her, speechless. How could life be so cruel? Had she been given someone to care for once again, only to find that she would soon be snatched away from her?

"You may be angry with me," Sophia went on, wiping her eyes. "I can always go back to the hotel. I will when it's close to the end. Or I'll take a studio apartment. That might be better, but I'm determined not to be a burden to anyone when . . . well, when it's time to die. I have that part of it all planned out, prepaid funeral arrangements, everything. But until then, I realize that I need someone. You saw that, didn't you, Jade?"

"I'm so sorry," Jade told her. If Sophia had ever become a mother, Jade thought, unlike *her* mother, she never would have abandoned her only child—not for any reason. Why should this good woman have to die? Life was so unfair. But she shouldn't go there. It was too painful, even now. Just as this was. Would it never come to an end, she asked herself? Thank God there was Wendy. Not that she would be able to tell her about

Sophia, but there would still be more and more time to spend with Wendy. Yes, somewhere in the midst of all of this, there was that to look forward to, something to hold on to.

There was nothing Jade could say except to tell Sophia that she would go along with whatever she wanted.

Sophia opened her eyes, searching deep into Jade's. "Maybe we can be a comfort to one another, what with both of us being alone in the world."

"Yes," Jade responded, returning her look, "I know we can."

Getting past that, with a sigh of relief, Sophia then urged Jade not to fuss over her. "You have a life besides me, Jade, please, go live it. I will be fine. I feel safe here, with you."

Despite the fullness of her days, there was a nebulous feeling about Jade's life right now, she realized soon after she had taken Sophia in. Was it simple restlessness? Loneliness? Was it anticipating the loss of Sophia? No. It was more than that. Amid caring for her, and maintaining the house, the daily routines of just being, there was something missing and she couldn't put a name to it. She had everything she had thought she'd yearned for: financial security and anonymity. Plus class, something she hadn't realized she wanted until meeting Wendy, who was finally back from Tuscany with tales of fabulous cuisine and trips through the gorgeous countryside, insisting that Jade would join her next trip. Time spent with her was always uplifting. She had grown to think like Wendy, to emulate her gestures, even the casually sophisticated way she dressed.

"When in doubt, wear black," she told Jade whenever they shopped the stores along Newbury Street, and she always followed her advice.

Beautiful, elegant, lively, opinionated—Wendy was always surprising Jade with adventures, like those tickets this past Saturday night to *La Bohème*, a thrill ever since Wendy had introduced her to opera, or the overnight trip to Vermont last fall, before Sophia's arrival, where Jade had reveled in autumn's last days of warmth, and the glory of fall foliage in full-blown display. It was a relief to spend time with Wendy, to escape the heavy feeling of disaster waiting right around the corner. Her life had been a series of disasters, although she yearned for all of them to be buried in the past. Don't think about them, she told herself, and they will evaporate.

Wendy had lived a fascinating life, a graduate from Wellesley with a Master's in Economics, a career in the world of finance with Smith Barney in New York, after which she had moved to Boston. She seemed to fill whatever space she occupied with an energy that was both intellectual and spiritual.

"Not always an exciting life, but a full one," she had told Jade. "Hey, I thought Bostonians were supposed to be friendly, but they're worse than New Yorkers. Thank goodness we met. Knowing you has made my day, as the saying goes."

Jade couldn't agree more. Unlike Josie and Sophia, Wendy was a sister. The friend that, other than Bear, she had never had.

Sunday, as when they first met, they were taking a long walk, a favorite outing, in the cool fall light that claimed the last days of September. Jade loved the chill air and the way the leaves had begun to scuttle along the sidewalks. And then there were the fall flowers, particularly the golden mums and the hydrangea blooms gone green and blue, drunk with their own juices.

Wendy was regaling her with the time when she had taken the Queen Elizabeth to Europe and thought she was being pursued on board by the most handsome and eligible young man. "Can you imagine how I felt when I found out that he was the resident gigolo?" she asked, giggling. "While I spent most of the return voyage throwing up, he was up on deck romancing some other unsuspecting girl."

Jade never tired of hearing Wendy's stories, and yet, she found herself resenting not having been part of that experience, all those years ago, and when they *were* together, although she refrained from asking, Jade was obsessed with how Wendy spent her time without her, envious of her many side trips with old friends. Coveting her friendship, she wanted Wendy all to herself.

CHAPTER THIRTY-SIX

Jade found Sophia to be a soft-spoken, gentle lady who never complained, in spite of any pain she might have been experiencing, and asked for little except to have Josie's comfy chair moved to her room where she spent most days by the window that opened to the back of the house. All through the summer and fall, Jade had felt her watching whenever she worked in the yard, pruning trees, mowing, raking, and weeding the flowerbeds.

"You know," Sophia said, one November afternoon when Jade was arranging mums in a vase, "I think I'm ready to leave. My time is coming."

Jade dropped the scissors and bent quickly to retrieve them, speaking from a crouched position, not wanting Sophia to see the fear in her face. Here comes the next disaster, she thought. I don't know if I can go through with "the plan."

"Not yet, Sophia," she exclaimed. "Are you in more pain? You promised you'd tell me when you felt worse."

"And you promised not to argue when it was time for me to move to a rental." Sophia reached forward to smooth Jade's hair back from her face. It felt like such a loving touch, Jade thought. "We discussed it and you agreed that I shouldn't die here in your home."

"Don't talk about dying," Jade told her angrily. "I won't let you."

"Please, Jade. Will you just make the arrangements? Soon?"

Jade thought of her second *assignment* in Rochester, with the Johnsons. "Auntie Georgia's" mother had been living with them up until she had developed bone cancer and was in screaming pain, then they had moved her to a nursing home. She could have hired an LPN, like me, for her mother, Jade thought, but the Johnsons were too busy with their careers. "There is nothing further we can do for her," "Auntie Georgia" had hissed angrily at her husband. "They can dope her up, and she'll just have to tough it through."

Regardless of the past, would I have wanted Mama to suffer if I knew she was mortally ill?

When she had first heard about Sophia's plan of dying alone, Jade had thought that it was something she would reconsider when the time came. But she understood now, knowing a lot about Sophia, that never once in her life had she, apparently, become a burden on someone else. And yet, before becoming ill, she'd lived in a hotel because she couldn't live independently. And then there was the pain. Jade knew enough about this particular cancer to know that there could be a great deal of it at the end, although she could make it easier for Sophia. There were ways; ways that Sophia had made it clear she knew, as well.

Right after Thanksgiving, Sophia rented a studio apartment in her name on Marlborough Street. A sublet fully furnished. A perfect location. Jade arranged for Sophia's medication to be delivered from the same pharmacy she had been using. All summer, Sophia had been stockpiling the morphine by taking less each time than had been prescribed. "Those are for later," she had said to Jade. "Please, just leave them there. I swear to you that I'm tolerating the pain, for now."

Not even four weeks later, the change in Sophia was frightening; her memories were released, day by day, like gentle rain. Jade could see the cancer sweeping through her, a narrowing of energy, her voice gradually fading, her mind traveling down roads that were no longer open to her. Occasionally, she'd tilt her head and Jade could see a recollection break the surface of her thoughts and spill into her face, like a sweep of brightness from a lighthouse. By then, Jade had actually moved in with Sophia, resting on the pull-out couch—not sleeping—ever alert to every nuance of movement and sound.

Christmas, the first one since Josie had died, had come and gone without ceremony. Jade thought of the decorations that languished in the basement—all of Bea's little handmade things. At first, she had meant to throw them out, but, why hadn't she? *Was she going to follow Josie's same traditions, out of respect . . . or regret? . . . or love?*

"Now, Jade, oh God, please, now." Sophia's voice was surprisingly strong through the darkness.

As a nurse, Jade had agreed to Sophia's plan, knowing so well the horrible pain and humiliation that would come with this kind of death, having witnessed it numerous times at Serene. But still, she had to force herself to go into the kitchen and pulverize twenty-two morphine tablets, and then mix them into a small amount of sugared milk.

Standing in the doorway, she thought of Josie, who had died with all of her treasures around her, including Jade, but didn't feel the comfort of knowing they were there; and here was Sophia, fully aware, in a stranger's apartment, dying with nothing personal around her, nothing that told of her life, but a bottle of lilac perfume. And Jade.

Gathering Sophia's shriveled body into a sitting position, she held the glass to her parched lips. When she settled back against the pillows, Sophia murmured, "My angel."

What are you thinking? Jade wondered as she sat by the bed, waiting. Are you frightened? Do you believe in God? The afterlife? The resurrection? What are your most treasured memories? Do you have regrets? Finally, finally, Sophia's body relaxed as she surrendered to the painless death she had longed for.

Leaning her head against the frosted glass of the narrow window in the small bedroom, Jade watched the January snow, silver and dark, building drifts on the sill as the sky deepened into cold, dark lead.

She knew that, when there was no response to tomorrow's pharmacy delivery, Sophia's body would be discovered. In the meantime, she removed any evidence that might lead back to her, leaving the envelope with Sophia's wishes in plain view. That had been their plan, one that Sophia had made her swear to.

"Goodbye, sweet woman," Jade said aloud as she stood over the bed. "May someone who loved you, be waiting."

Would she, Jade wondered, ever be lucky enough to have that happen to her?

CHAPTER THIRTY-SEVEN

The temperature during Bear's early morning run was twelve degrees above zero, and by eight a.m., after the call came from Yvonne about a body having been discovered in an apartment on Marlborough Street, it had risen only two degrees. A harsh wind was blowing off the river from the north and Bear's hair whipped fitfully about his hatless head as he approached his car. Impatient to get going, he took a few moments to scrape just enough ice from the windshield to make a small opening and after struggling to get the door open, he got in and roared the engine to life. From Soldiers Field Road, he could see across the Charles River, frozen and snow-covered, scored with cross-country ski tracks.

By the time he reached Marlborough Street, the commuter traffic had picked up; exhausts plumed in the freezing air. Lappas was waiting in front of the building, hands buried under his armpits, and stamping his feet.

"It's about time," he grouched.

"I'm early," Bear told him.

It was 8:23 by the old woman's bedside clock. She was lying peacefully on her back as if asleep, and the phone

was off the hook. Probably, Bear thought, she had tried
to call someone in her last moments. Either that or she
had knocked it off the nightstand when she reached for
something.

"What d'ya you think, Kuruk, murder, suicide, or au
naturel?" Lappas asked Bear.

"Can't tell anything, yet. Get the M.E. over here and
a statement from the super."

"Yes sir, oh partner of few words," Lappas said.

Bear then turned to the young delivery boy from
the CVS pharmacy who anxiously explained that
Mrs. Markeha had been a customer for a number of
years.

"I used to make deliveries to her at the Copley Plaza,
and then a nurse started picking them up for a while,"
he explained. "And about a month ago, Mrs. Markeha
started to have deliveries here. That's all I know."

"Okay. I'll need a statement from you later," Bear told
him dismissively.

"She was a nice lady," the boy said to his retreating
back.

As Bear looked around the modest one-bedroom
apartment, it seemed obvious that the old woman, who,
he figured, had been in her late-eighties early-nineties
had lived alone. There were a number of medicine bottles
in the bathroom and empty ones on the nightstand along
with a sealed envelope addressed to "The Authorities," all
of which, with gloved hands, Bear bagged for the lab. The
labels read Sophia Markeha, at this address. The deceased,
as well as the entire apartment, was being photographed
while the techs searched the closets and drawers.

"Just an old lady, giving up the ship," Lappas said.
"That's my guess. There's no reason to search for clues,
since, given her age, there's little reason to think she has

been murdered. Of course, there's always suicide, which is the easy way out and usually packs a message: *see how I love you,* or, *see what you made me do.*"

"Maybe," Bear told him, "but as I see it, suicide is anger, coupled with despair."

On their way to the pharmacy on Commonwealth Avenue, they turned left past the Ritz. Across the street in the public garden, Washington sat astride his enormous horse draped with snow.

"That poor bastard must be freezing his balls off." Lappas always laughed at his own comments. Bear, as usual, hardly cracked a smile still thinking about the body of the old woman they had left behind them. At least she had apparently died peacefully, but he knew that they had to follow up, all the same. Poor woman. Dying alone. Although perhaps death is not the worst thing in the light of loss, he thought, a loss so achingly sad that, at times, it was almost unbearable.

They strode through CVS to the back and waited, not too patiently, for the pharmacist on duty to be free. Getting right to the point after explaining that Mrs. Markeha had died, Bear asked her why there were different doctors' names on the deceased's prescriptions.

"Mrs. Sophia Markeha is . . . was, a dear little lady. She's been a customer for several years and was very poor. Whenever she was sick, she'd go to Emergency at the Beth Israel Medical Center and take any doctor who was on duty. Even after being diagnosed with cancer, she did the same thing. "

"Was the morphine always delivered to her?"

Lappas started to say something, probably to remind him that the delivery kid had already answered that question, when Bear silenced him with a sharp wave of his hand.

"No, there were about six or eight months when her nurse picked them up."

"Do you have her name and where I can contact her?"

"Actually, no. She came with Mrs. Markeha so many times in the beginning that I knew her by sight. She always signed the book: "*for Sophia Markeha.*" God, have I done something terribly wrong, a professional error?"

"No, we're not concerned with that. Can you describe this nurse?"

"Yes. She is tall and slim, about late twenties. Long dark hair that she usually wore in a ponytail. Nice smile. Always pleasant. You could tell that they were friends. Oh, now I remember," the pharmacist added, "I think Mrs. Markeha called her Jane."

The morning seemed even colder when Bear and Lappas left CVS; a ragged cutting cold, like barbed wire.

CHAPTER THIRTY-EIGHT

Jade judged the progress of the storm by the thickness of the blanket that was accumulating in the backyard; ripples and hillocks covering small bushes, including an azalea she had protected with an upturned trash barrel and a burlap bag.

In the hush that comes upon a house when snow falls in the world outside, Jade's life was peaceful. Or should be. Why did she feel so haunted by loss? Yes, she'd had more than her share of it, only now, she reminded herself, there was Wendy to look forward to. Wendy was her future.

But these days, it came back to Sophia. Listed on the obituary page in the *Globe*, Jade, with great sadness, found the following notice: "Sophia Markeha came to her death by ingesting an overdose of pain medication prescribed for cancer, with suicidal intent. She leaves no apparent assets or heirs."

No mention of me, thank God.

Although she hadn't known her that long, less than a year, losing Sophia had had more of an impact than she would have imagined. And it had nothing to do with that money. Sophia had rapidly become an intimate part of her life. *She was such a lady.*

Re-reading the note from Sophia that Jade had found a few days later at the bottom of the oatmeal box, her throat went dry. God only knows when Sophia had put it there.

To My Angel, I dare not question what I did to merit having you come into my life. I never accomplished anything spectacular—I'm not special, I just tried to meet each day with optimism and sincerity. I have always tried to reach out along this long road I have traveled, to those less fortunate than myself. Maybe that is why it has come back to me, ten-fold . . .

We never talked about it, but I sense that you had been deeply hurt during your childhood and that even today, you believe that you do not deserve happiness. I assure you that no one deserves it more than you, Jade. Please, consider the contents of the "black bag" to be yours. Use it to provide security and to follow your dreams.

I thank you and my lucky stars for opening your home and your heart, and for keeping the promise, yet to come, that you solemnly made to me.

With all my love,

Sophia Markeha

Jade studied the handwriting written in small, formal script. Just like Sophia, clear in purpose, and loving. Somehow, Jade was certain that if Josie's mind had been clear at the end, she would have said something like that to her, just as she had during the years they spent together.

Financially, she was more than secure, but whatever else she had done, Jade had never cared about profiting from the death of these women. And now there was so much money. Maybe she should find another woman in need. Or a worthy charity.

It was, she realized, terrible to care about someone and not take part in laying her to rest, as when she had made arrangements for Josie's funeral, following closely the instructions Josie had made while she was in good health—that she wanted to be cremated and to have her ashes spread around the "lovely" gardens that Jade had created for her around her home. Somehow, by following her wishes, Jade had managed to blank out those last months of dementia, and remember Josie as the mother she had always needed so badly.

Because of the circumstances under which Sophia had chosen to die, Jade had had to say goodbye to her when she left the Marlborough Street apartment without knowing whether or not whoever found her would treat her with the respect she deserved and follow her wishes in regard to burial arrangements. Somehow, Jade thought, February seemed to be a suitable month for dying when everything outside was dead; the trees black and frozen, the snow unrelentingly cold.

Funerals. Had there been one for little Angie? Or Beaknose? That timeline was a complete blur, and as far as Papa's death, not the gradual one he'd sustained in that nursing home in Rochester, but the final one about which Jade had not been informed. Not that she had cared at the time. Mama was probably dead by now, too.

Not counting Wendy, *thank God for Wendy,* she didn't have another friend in this world. She realized, finally, that the Rochester "Aunties" had actually given her something extremely valuable . . . the drive to become a nurse. For that, she was grateful; it gave her a purpose, something she could always fall back on.

Gently prodding her soon after they'd met, Sophia had asked if she had a beau, to which she had answered that there had been a boy in high school, and after him, she could never love again. What she couldn't tell her was that a boyfriend now might open up parts of herself she didn't want to know. She had no desire to date and no illusions about falling in love.

Now, she was almost thirty. Of course she had thought about having a child, even without being married, but what kind of a mother would she be with Mama and all the "Aunties" in Rochester as role models? How could she be certain that she wouldn't have done the same thing that Mama did . . . just walk away and leave her child, unloved, unprotected? No, she did not want a child or a husband. Jade had learned how to take care of people, but not how to love them unconditionally as Josie had her daughter. She felt a new understanding of just how devastated Josie must have felt when Bea had died.

Was it her fate, she wondered, to die as much alone as both Sophia and Josie would have done had it not been for her? If only she had not lost Bear so soon. There could have been a marriage. Children.

But, that hadn't happened. Now everything depended on her friendship with Wendy. Nothing must happen to that because if it did, Jade was not at all certain what she would do.

✧ ✧ ✧

That Thursday, as Wendy set out two gold-rimmed cups and saucers of her delicate bone china, she asked Jade what was the matter.

"I've lost a special client—actually, a friend," she said, taken by surprise that Wendy had read her mood so well. "Someone that I was very fond of."

When Wendy put her hand on her arm, and said, "tell me," Jade began to cry. It began like a small stab of pain, deep in her gut, and turned into a great heaving. The grief came pouring out of her.

Later, some time after Jade's sobs had subsided; they sat together in the quiet, as the snow fell softly outside the window, filling the room with crisp evening light.

"Hey, we don't need to be held hostage by winter from Thanksgiving to Easter," Wendy said suddenly, breaking the silence with a loud voice and jumping to her feet. "Let's go on vacation for a couple of weeks. My treat. I know a marvelous resort in Mexico called The Riviera Maya. It's *the* place to rest and be pampered. I haven't been there recently, but I remember it as a great getaway with lots of atmosphere. What do you think, Jade?"

"Well, I've never been out of the country, but . . ."

"I consider that a *yes*. I'll make the reservations, we'll get you a passport, and then we'll go shopping for bathing suits," Wendy said with a conspiratorial grin.

Jade decided to lean back and let Wendy do it all. She wanted to start over again, to be someone living happily in the world, not someone hidden away behind secrets and pain. She felt a calmness descend upon her, a quietness on the far side of thinking. She liked to watch her friend whenever she sprang into action. *She's almost thirty years older than I am, yet she has more energy and optimism than I'll ever have.* Besides, she was tired, at least for now, of taking care of people. Now she was the one who needed to be taken care of, and the luxury of having found someone who wanted to do that was an unbearable relief.

She must never lose Wendy. Never.

CHAPTER THIRTY-NINE

"Back to reality," Wendy commented, while they waited, shivering, for a cab outside Logan's American Airlines terminal.

"How can I ever thank you," Jade said, as they sped toward the Sumner Tunnel. "You couldn't have picked a better place to vacation. I was so amazed by how warm the Caribbean Sea actually felt, warm enough for even *me* to swim. And the sandy beach, it just went on for miles."

"What did you enjoy the most?" Wendy asked between yawns.

"The trip to Cozumel, the spa, the . . . everything, I guess. Just being with you Wendy."

"What I got a kick out of was when you realized that "European-style sunbathing" meant nudes on the beaches," Wendy told her. "Your look of surprise was priceless."

"Ha ha, very funny," Jade said, "but I really did love the Mexican people; they were so welcoming."

Resting her head against the back of the seat, Jade sighed contentedly. "And the hotel," she exclaimed. "I've never known such luxury, or eaten so much. It was all so special. I had more fun than I have ever had in my life, Wendy, thanks to you. I'll never forget this."

"The feeling is mutual, dear," Wendy said. "But frankly, I'm pooped. I'm afraid my traveling days are done. I'm not as young as you, kiddo."

Surprised by her friend's comment, Jade reminded herself of their age span, and was certain that she would feel differently after some down time.

Arriving at Pinckney Street, Wendy stepped out of the cab and after pointing out which luggage was hers to the driver, she then leaned into the back seat.

"I didn't want to tell you until after this trip, Jade, but I'm moving to Florida," Wendy said, casually, as if she were predicting tomorrow's weather. "Remember Linda, the woman I went to the Caribbean with last year? Well, she wants me to share a condo with her in St. Pete Beach, and I've decided to do it. Just think, you can come and visit us sometime."

And with that, she was gone—leaving Jade feeling as though someone had delivered a body blow that had left her breathless.

No! No! She nearly screamed the word out loud.

Wendy cannot leave her.

I won't let her.

Putting on her dark glasses and steeling herself to be quiet until they reached Park Square, Jade leaned forward, tapped the driver on the shoulder, and told him to stop by the entrance to the subway.

After that, taking another cab as far as a restaurant on Newbury Street, she left her single piece of luggage tucked under a vanity in the ladies' room, and walked up the hill to Wendy's apartment.

CHAPTER FORTY

Bostonians, exhibiting their customary resilience, were out on the streets as usual, stepping over icy curbs, maneuvering around snowdrifts, shoveling out cars blocked in by snowplows that had worked throughout the night.

When Bear and Lappas arrived on the scene, the crime scene investigators were already taking prints off the door. The murder victim, as would be reported later in the news, was wearing only a bra and panties, sprawled in a grotesque posture of lifelessness, part of her skull ripped away, Bear surmised, by a 9mm semi-automatic handgun. Two spent shells lay on the floor beside what was left of her. Overkill for such close range. He noticed that her blood had soaked into the rich reds and blues of the oriental carpet where clumps of her long hair had pulled loose from a bun and lay caked in a wide puddle that had spread under her head. The techs were taking blood smears and nail clippings. Bear, bending down to take a closer look at the victim, noticed a rape kit on the floor. The terrible silence of her limbs made him clench his teeth while a myriad of questions raced through his mind. He hated the profound indifference of death, especially a violent one like this.

Proceeding into the bedroom where the forensic team was collecting evidence with tweezers, using little envelopes for their findings, he found that every bureau drawer had been dumped onto the floor, clothes yanked out of the closets, and that a large standing jewelry chest with at least a dozen drawers had been completely emptied onto the floor.

"The perp probably thought she wasn't home," Lappas said, standing in the doorway. "Must've panicked and gone berserk when he saw her. Doesn't look like he had the time to actually take anything. Pretty much open-and-shut about motive, seems to me. Robbery gone bad, plain and simple. Very bad."

"I wonder who heard the shots," Bear said, ignoring his partner's conclusion. "Who called it in?"

Lappas shrugged. "No one heard anything as far as we know. A neighbor called it in. He was on the way to work and saw that the door was ajar."

"That's odd, at five in the morning," Bear said. "Did he come in? Did he touch anything?"

"No. People watch too much TV these days to make that mistake."

"He could be lying."

"Shit," Lappas said.

Although Lappas kept talking, Bear scarcely listened. Another day on the Boston Police Force. Another brutal crime. Would life have been different if that incident in the woods back in Rochester so many years ago had never happened? But, he reminded himself, he had had no choice then because he had loved Jade. He supposed he loved her still.

And then, forcing himself back to the present, he proceeded to begin the business of solving a crime committed against a total stranger.

That evening, after a quick shower, Bear put on jeans, a blue dress shirt, and a wool pullover sweater before knocking down a double scotch and slipping on his parka. He was going to meet Lappas and Yvonne at Locke-Ober's raw bar for drinks and appetizers.

Even though it was still snowing, he decided to walk since it would probably be impossible to find a place to park. Even so, he loved this city . . . Boston, where the garbage man was the sanitary engineer and a prostitute was a sex counselor. All the poverty and suffering now covered by snow.

The hard slanting wind soon caught up with him. He shoved his fists into his coat pockets and hunched his shoulders to cover his neck, the bulge of his shoulder holster snug on the left side of his body. Somehow, he couldn't get this morning's homicide out of his mind. *That poor, unsuspecting woman.* He wondered if she had a family. So far, no one had found anyone to contact. He knew he would have to go back to the apartment, just as he so often did.

Even after the evidence had been collected and the crime scene tapes had been removed, something inexplicable took him back to the scene of any murder he had investigated. He would stand in the center of the living room, the bedroom, or a rooftop—wherever—to absorb the essence of it, breathe it deeply into his lungs, have it become part of him, for only then could he hope to understand it.

The minute he walked through the popular but expensive restaurant with its turn-of-the-century décor, directly to the lounge where it was more casual and less expensive, Yvonne started waving to him. Catching the attention of a nearby waitress, Bear ordered a double scotch sent to their table.

"I was just telling Yvonne some of the details about the robbery on the Hill," Lappas said, pushing a bowl of pretzels toward Bear.

"My God, what is the matter with people?" Yvonne demanded, twirling a bracelet, absently, around her wrist. "To kill for the sake of some jewelry or whatever? It really gets me. Babies slammed against a wall. A pregnant woman kicked in the belly last week, and that drive-by shooting. Now another innocent victim. If people like this are being killed, if nobody gives a damn anymore, if someone can murder a child or a nice old lady, it's—it's almost more than I can take."

Bear was afraid that she was going to burst into tears, but Lappas seemed, as usual, unconcerned.

"Psychos, junkies, and whores; the world is full of them, ready to do things for a buck that would turn most people's stomachs," he said, as he tilted his chair back so he could glance at the TV behind the bar. "It's love or money. As far as I'm concerned, those are the only motives for murder."

Yvonne took a swallow of her Canadian Club, and slammed the glass onto the table. "Or insanity."

"What about passion or fear?" Bear added, finally warm enough to slip off his parka, but could feel the wetness that had seeped into his boots.

"That, too," they both agreed. Yvonne's face, crazed with freckles, was flushed.

Bear charged after the waitress and ordered another round and a platter from the raw bar. Now he was sweating. As usual, he couldn't stop thinking about the crime scene. Each one haunted him until they were resolved.

Two hours later, Yvonne and Lappas headed back to their respective apartments, leaving Bear, who, having decided not to wait until morning, made his way to Beacon Hill and the scene of the latest fatality. Turning on all the lights, he sat on the edge of the couch and stared at the chalked outline of the woman's figure on the bloodstained carpet. What had she endured in that awful moment of realization that she was probably going to die? Had she begged her murderer just to take what he wanted, and promise that she would never identify him? Had she screamed for mercy? Who was she thinking about just before the shot rang out? *Why did she have to die?*

After making a tour of the apartment, which had obviously been thoroughly searched, he returned to the living room and proceeded to go through the papers on the desk until he came upon an envelope entitled LAST WILL AND TESTAMENT. Taking the envelope into the kitchen with him, Bear checked the cupboards for liquor. *Ah! Scotch. Chivas.* Not bothering with ice or a glass, he used a paper towel to pick up the bottle, returned to the living room, and making himself comfortable on the velvet couch, proceeded to read: *I, Wendy Feinberg, of Suffolk County, Massachusetts, being of sound mind, do hereby declare this to be my Last Will and Testament, hereby revoking all former wills made by me.*

All of my estate, real, personal, or mixed, I do give, devise, and bequeath to my dear friend, Jade Gerard.

The paper fluttered from Bear's hand onto his lap. He was stunned. He felt as though he had fallen to the bottom of a deep well, and was hearing a faint voice calling to him from above.

Jade Gerard . . . Jade Gerard . . . Could it be?

Jade.

CHAPTER FORTY-ONE

From her bedroom window, Jade saw that it had begun to snow—heavy, wet flakes quickly covering the frozen ground that had been ridged like a scrub board. They had, she thought, made it home just in time. Glancing at her watch, she sat up quickly, confused to see that it said Tuesday. What happened to Monday? They came back Sunday night. *Could I have slept an entire day away?*

Wrapped in Josie's faded chenille bathrobe, which always seemed to comfort her no matter what, she hurried down to the kitchen. After refilling the bird feeder on the back deck, Jade carried a steaming cup of coffee upstairs where she unpacked her suitcase, separating her light and dark clothes for the laundry.

What an absolutely incredible time they had had together; swimming, sunbathing, eating exotic food. How could Wendy even *consider* throwing away their friendship to go and live in Florida?

In spite of the residual exhilaration of their trip together, Jade felt a downward pull, a heaviness to her step. Their vacation must have tired her more than she had thought, losing an entire day to sleep. Having just showered and dressed, she was thinking of dropping by Wendy's on her way to the Boston Public Library to return a book she had read on their trip, when, abruptly, there came a loud knock on her front door, bringing with it a strange, powerful sense of foreboding. Suddenly, the day had changed, like the direction of a squall on the horizon. A chill ran down her spine as the knock sounded again.

"Yes?" she said, opening the door just a crack.

"Homicide Detective Mike Lappas, ma'am," the officer said, flashing his badge. "Are you Jade Gerard?"

"Yes, what is it? What's wrong?" *Why? Why is he here? Oh, no, it's about what I did for Sophia. Or the man in the hotel? It couldn't be about stinking Manny, could it?*

"Well, ma'am, do you know a Wendy Feinberg?"

"My God," Jade exclaimed. "Has something happened to her?"

"She has met an untimely death . . ."

Death? Jade slammed the door. *Death? Wendy?* She pressed her lips together, but the cries kept pushing up from her chest and into her throat, like the screams of an injured animal. The damn cop kept knocking, calling her name.

"Go away."

"I believe you're the closest thing to family. I need to talk to you," he called through the door.

"Not now!" she heard herself shriek. "Go away. Tell me later. I can't . . . ."

The rest of the day passed in a daze of denial. And when at last she slept, she dreamed of being in an airport. The plane had landed and her mother came down the ramp. Although her face looked like Wendy's, she was definitely Mama. She was wearing a flowered organdy dress with a full, flowing skirt that fluttered about her ankles as she walked. Jade ran to her, but she didn't recognize her own daughter, even after Jade told her who she was. "No," she said over and over again, "I never had a daughter." Then Jade dreamed that she was drowning and that Wendy was peering through the water, waving goodbye.

Jade woke with a start. Why was it that she had returned last night to see her friend? She couldn't remember now, and besides, it was two nights ago. Everything was such a blur. And why had she left her luggage at that restaurant on Newbury? The only thing she *could* remember was picking it up and calling a cab to take her home.

Wendy. Wendy . . .

What had the police officer said? An untimely death?

What did that mean? Had Wendy been struck by a car? A stroke?

But no. He must have meant someone else. She was fine just yesterday . . . no, it had been the day before. She had seen her going into her building, hadn't she?

He must be wrong.

So why did she suddenly remember—oh so vividly—that first chicken she had had to kill?

And the blood when she had chopped off its head.

More blood than she had ever seen before or since.

CHAPTER FORTY-TWO

"What did she say?" Bear asked Lappas when he returned to the car.

"Come back later. Jesus! After she slammed the door in my face, I could hear her screaming."

"All right. We'll come back later. She's not going anywhere. Give her a little time."

"She'll see it in the news, anyway." Then Lappas turned to Bear and asked, "Well, do you think she's the one you used to know?" Bear could tell that he was dying of curiosity.

"Maybe," Bear told him, "although I didn't get much of a look."

But of course it was her. He'd known it the minute he read the victim's will. Bear couldn't believe that Jade, his Jade, had suddenly reentered his life—that their paths had crossed again after all this time. He had given up his search years ago, but never his longing.

✳ ✳ ✳

Later that afternoon, perhaps sooner than protocol would dictate, but well before the day was over, Bear sent Lappas for the ME report, and found himself again in Jade's driveway. The house was a traditional Colonial in the '60s style, but impeccably maintained, the shrubs along the front protected by wooden frames from winter damage.

Although there were lights on in a room at the back of the house, no one answered his knock. Was she, he wondered, so deeply in denial about her friend's death that she intended to isolate herself? Even more important, was this woman really Jade? He waited after knocking on the door several times. He knew she was in there. Even though he was breaking all the rules, when he discovered that the door had swung slightly ajar, he let himself into the darkened hall.

"Hello? Ms. Gerard?" his voice unfurled up the stairs. As he spoke, Bear made his way toward what must be the lighted kitchen, his badge for identification ready to use if he had been wrong about her. "I'm from the Boston homicide department. My partner was here earlier. I need to talk to you."

And then, there she was! His Jade. Tall, long-limbed, still athletic-looking, with loose chestnut hair about her drawn face, thinner than he remembered it, and skin the color of cream. She was watching a small TV that sat on the kitchen counter. The sound was off, and a news commentator was obviously reporting on yesterday's murder. When she turned her gaze toward him, her eyes were swollen and red, but there was no denying the green of them. Without a doubt, it was Jade.

"Bear?" she cried his name, and swayed, her face frozen, a wide-eyed mask of confusion. "I don't understand."

He approached her carefully, as if she was a bird he might startle into flight. Taking hold of her arm, he led her to a chair at the breakfast table, gently pushing down on her shoulders until she was seated. All color was drained from her face. He pulled another chair around next to hers for himself, and then, softly, quietly, told her about his life, his work, and how he had happened on her name and guessed, no, *hoped*, that it might, in the face of every improbability, be her. He had picked up a pencil from the table and stared at it, twirling it between his fingers as he spoke.

He explained, as in the end he had to, what had happened to her friend and that in her will, which he had found in Wendy's desk, she had left everything to Jade.

"That was what led me to you," he told her.

She stared at him without comprehension, just as she had when he told her the principal's demands that day when his life with her had seemed to come to an end forever.

"I don't want her things," she cried. "No. I don't deserve anything from her."

He watched Jade get up, then walk over to the window and poke one finger aimlessly in a flowerpot. Bear tried to take her hand, but she yanked it back as though he had burned her. He could almost see the sorrow rise like a wave inside her as her chest caved and her shoulders shook. She crossed her arms, pressing her fingernails into her flesh. Her lips were quivering.

They stood together, wordless, as dusk dropped quickly into the room.

CHAPTER FORTY-THREE

Now there was just the pain, except on rare occasions when she managed to sleep. Often, she rose in the middle of the night to sit on her deck where the cold made her numb. The days compressed, one into another and she passed through them, trapped in forgetfulness and confusion.

Numbness had propelled her through the funeral. Although Bear had told her that he had no experience with such things, he had taken charge and made the arrangements. At first, he had tried to pass plans by Jade, but she had not been capable of either agreeing or disagreeing. Her most coherent thoughts centered on Bear. *Who was he? How had he happened to come back into her life?*

The only guidance she had given him was that she wanted Wendy's ashes spread under the purple smoke tree in her backyard. When Wendy had discussed the "what ifs" of her own death, Jade had never thought that it would happen so soon. She had buried the urn that held Josie's ashes in the lily-of-the-valley flowerbed that, later in the summer, also displayed masses of perennial forget-me-nots, a site that Josie had suggested before her mind had given way.

"I can pick up the ashes right after a meeting I have to go to," Bear said now, "and still be here by three. Would that be all right with you?" Bear's question startled her.

Why was he being so nice? He didn't even know Wendy. And he doesn't know me. Not anymore.

✳ ✳ ✳

The afternoon of the funeral, when Bear rang the doorbell, the house looked as if it had been vacated, all the shades pulled down to the sills. When she opened the door, Jade was still in her pajamas, her hair disheveled. Walking past him to a closet, wordlessly, she put on a coat. He found boots in the hall and when he slipped them on her feet, she placed her hand on his back to steady herself. He seemed to understand that she was doing the best that she could.

She fumbled with the zipper. "I can't do this," she said, staring at the floor.

"Yes, you can," he said, pushing past her, out to the deck. He held the door open. "Come."

They were the only people at Wendy Feinberg's funeral.

The sky that had been overcast all morning had turned into rain with a cold, cutting edge to it, casting a pall of desolation over everything. Wendy's ashes, scattered at the base of the tree, blended with the rain into deep iron grays.

"You can't understand," she told him. "Wendy was everything to me. I cannot imagine her being gone from my life."

He asked no questions. She had known that he would not. Not now. Perhaps never. He only said, "I'm here for you now, Jade. I never thought I'd find you, and yet this wonderful friend of yours, in the saddest way, has brought us back together. We can at least be grateful for that."

"I know." She stood there a long time, trembling. A dog was barking somewhere in the neighborhood. She looked up at him, the rain beading in his black hair.

Returning to the house, they both slipped out of their soaked coats and kicked off their soggy, muddy shoes. And then, when, without ceremony, Bear pulled her close, the liquid ache inside her took her to the very edges of the grief that was coming for her. She let herself relax in his arms.

Wordlessly, Jade led the way upstairs to her bedroom, where they lay together for some time, her head on his chest, his hand stroking her tangled hair.

"Shh, shh," he kept saying until they both fell asleep. "Shh. Everything will be all right."

CHAPTER FORTY-FOUR

Nearly a week after the funeral, her sorrow came to her, sweet and familiar. She bent under it, tears thickened in her throat and she began, at last, to weep. What was it Wendy had always said? *When one door closes, another door opens.* Of course, she had been thinking about their relationship, how Jade had blossomed. And then, in the face of that, what had she done?—abandon her—just as Mama had.

She tried to consider her options; do this, do that, or decide not to decide now. It was always an option to just go on as she had been. When she was feeling needy and alone as she did now, when she ached with longing, these words appeared before her: *I am an orphan.* Dreams fell away in the face of exhaustion.

There was nothing but gardens below her bedroom window, a long rectangle of perennial color that she had created for Josie—all of it overgrown now and too obvious, like some gaudy happiness that had become completely foreign to her.

At the end of each day, Bear showed up at her door, almost always with something to eat. His kindness, the way he touched her, held her hand, was almost heartbreaking. But he kept the conversation light, and left before ten each evening. Jade knew he was patiently waiting—waiting for what, though? For sex? For her to confess her sins?

Last week he had asked if she'd like to go for a hike and picnic in New Hampshire, where they'd both grown up. Didn't he know that no such place existed for her? And in the same breath, he suggested that she start doing some yard work—clean up her flowerbeds. Would she like him to mow the yard?

No. She can mow the grass herself, just like always. She can do everything by herself. She didn't need anyone anymore.

✻ ✻ ✻

On a glorious early morning near the end of May, Jade rose from her bed, dressed for gardening, ate a large bowl of Cheerios with raisins and slices of banana, followed by coffee and an English muffin with peanut butter, and then spent the day working outside, aware of how wonderful it was to plunge her hands deep in the sun-warmed soil, to pull weeds and dead leaves from the flowerbed and to feel alive again.

Mid-afternoon, Jade put away her gardening tools, went into the house, and took a long, hot shower. When Bear pulled in the driveway, she was sitting on the front step, dressed in jeans and a T-shirt, drying her hair in the sun. He flashed a huge smile and she knew that, just as she had expected, he was relieved to see her, at long last, out of her pajamas. Wendy had recited another saying when Jade had refused to reveal anything about her past: *Today is the beginning of the rest of your life.* Now, here was Bear, returned after all these years, beginning where he'd left off, taking care of her. Protecting her from harm.

If she had only known, the idea of losing Wendy might not have been so devastating, so completely unacceptable.

He had a box with La Primavera written on the top, and, remembering how delicious the food at that North End restaurant was, her mouth began to water. For the first time in weeks she was actually hungry. How incredible and sad it was that Wendy's death had brought her and Bear together. *Although, Wendy would have loved the twist, the coincidence. She would have called it fate.*

After dinner, they carried their wine glasses and the remaining bottle of Chianti onto the back deck and sat in the stillness of the evening. Swallows dipped and darted in the air like shadows, feeding on the insects hovering in the fading light, and the silence between them became heavy with the weight of years. They had a connection that could only have been forged in childhood, the sort of connection that happens once in a lifetime. Definitely only once—for these two orphans.

Slowly, Bear stood and pulled Jade to her feet. And when he put his hands on either side of her face, his eyes intense and unreadable, she felt a warm sensation spread upward from her belly. Rising on her tiptoes, she kissed him, whispering "Bear," to which he made an inarticulate sound. And then suddenly he was kissing her, pulling her close and slanting his mouth across hers as she wrapped her arms around his neck, melting into him. Miraculously, it was as if some dark and heavy spirit had left her body. At long last, she felt free.

His mouth left hers to feather-kiss along the line of her jaw. "You're more beautiful than ever," he whispered against her skin. He raised his head to look down at her. The tenderness in his eyes was enough to make her catch her breath, to smile a secret smile. They kissed again with an urgency that made her dizzy. The first stars were out already and night was falling.

This time, Bear led the way to her bedroom, closed the blinds, and put their world on hold. She wanted to believe that Wendy, if she had lived, would have been happy that she had been reunited with Bear. If only she hadn't planned, behind Jade's back, to leave her, to go to Florida with a friend, someone that was obviously far more important to her than Jade. *She deserved this happiness after what everyone had done to her.*

The next morning, just as the sun was still no more than a silvery light in the east, just for a few minutes bright with possibility, Jade turned her face toward the window. Bear had left during the night, but she was content to be alone. She couldn't believe this feeling of hope welling from deep inside her; something she never thought she deserved or that would ever come her way. Slipping out of bed, she ran down the stairs and opened the front door to stand for a minute, breathing in the early morning air, watching a sparrow hop delicately along a fence, an ounce of brown feather and black bib. God's eye was on it.

Could God's eye be on her, finally, even in spite of what she had done?

CHAPTER FORTY-FIVE

When Bear tapped the horn as he pulled into the driveway, Jade, looking like a young girl in her jean shorts and a crisp white blouse, came running out of the house, grinning, with a cooler in hand and a backpack over her shoulder. He liked the grace with which she still carried herself. He'd never forgotten that.

"Did you decide where we're going?" she asked, throwing her things on the back seat.

"We're hiking Mount Monadnock," he told her. "That's what the Abenaki Indians called it. It means, mountain that stands alone."

"I like that. It reminds me of you."

For the next hour, they rode in a comfortable silence along roads lined with trees that grew so close to it that the branches overlapped to cover it like a canopy, casting lacy patterns of shadows on the asphalt.

In the cool, pine-scented woods, they filled their lungs as they climbed past weeds and thistles, rust-brown leaves, red boxberries, and lichen-covered rocks. Bear watched Jade, strong and resilient, reach for saplings to pull herself up with the casual vitality of an athlete, and laughed when one snapped off in her hand. Once he caught her before she slipped backwards, and held her tight, nuzzling his face in her neck. She turned in the circle of his arms and they kissed until voices rose from the trail below.

Farther up the winding trail, Jade stretched out flat, resting on star-tipped moss where mist settled on a mountain stream, and drank from the freezing water while Bear held her hair back from her face. Then, he slipped his hand into the rushing olive-green water and chose a satin stone.

"This is for that memory box of yours," he said, as he handed it to her. "Your retreat box. You see, I remember everything."

She held the stone in her hand as though it was a diamond. He wondered if Jade found it strange to be hiking a mountain together in a state in which they'd both grown up, neither one mentioning that wretched time in that wretched town. That was then, he told himself. This was now.

When they reach the treeless summit, they were greeted by a 360-degree view that stretched far into the distance. The wind whipped around the peak, and blew Jade's hair across her face, filling her blouse like a kite.

"You're looking at the states of Vermont and Massachusetts," Bear told her, "and even as far as the White Mountains on really clear days." She believed in him with her eyes; he knew this by the careful way she listened to him.

"Breathtaking," she said, reaching for his hand, leaning against him. She was pink with exertion, her cheeks were flushed and lovely. He inhaled her scent.

Settling down with their picnic, they watched kids climbing over big slabs and boulders. Someone behind them was saying that Mount Monadnock is the second most hiked mountain in the world after Fuji in Japan. They smiled together at hearing that pronouncement.

And then, suddenly, a cloud passed in front of the sun making them both shiver, as a flock of crows flew high above them, screeching in foreboding cries.

CHAPTER FORTY-SIX

It was an overcast Sunday morning in mid-July when Bear awoke to feel the warmth of Jade's body next to his. Often, when they were in bed together, he felt as if she had been fused to him. He loved her legs, her arms, and most of all, her hands—surprisingly strong for someone her size. Was this the kind of falling in love that they had dreamed of in high school? Love had never been declared to him so passionately, without reserve.

At first, their conversations had merely touched on the surface of things, and, for the time being, Bear was satisfied that Jade was not willing to delve any deeper into the past than that. Just to have found her was enough. Or so he told himself, until certain questions became so important that he could no longer pretend that they did not exist. His training as a detective told him that she was withholding secrets that she was not yet ready to share with him. Maybe dark, destructive secrets.

Later, when they had just finished eating breakfast, he found himself asking her who Josephine Gerard was, and she simply stared at him, expressionless, making no response.

"Well?" he pressed, knowing that, to Jade, the question was out of left field. "Why are you using her last name and where is she now?" She didn't answer, and they sat for what seemed to Bear a long time, the silence gathering between them.

Suddenly, she was staring at him with eyes he no longer recognized. "A woman I used to work for. And if you already know," she said, "and I think you do, why are you asking?"

Bear knew from experience that when someone went immediately on the defensive, that there was a lot more to their story and it needed to be pried out of them.

"She's dead, isn't she?" he said.

"Yes, she died some years ago after adopting me. Why are you checking up on my past?" Jade's voice was harsh and he could see that she was leaning back, pulling away from him, from some swirling undercurrent; probably from her own fear of what might be coming.

"Because, that's what detectives do," he told her, with a little smile that he hoped would lower the bar. "So, have you changed your name more than once?"

She started to fidget with the sugar bowl, then, picking up a spoon to scoop some out, she slowly poured it back into the bowl. Over and over again.

Bear warned himself not to go too fast. He had seen her laid low by Wendy's death, and he did not want to be responsible for propelling her into that kind of state again. But then, excuses aside, he knew that he had to find out the truth.

"Were you—have you been married?" he asked. "Is that where Gerard comes from?"

"No and no."

"I didn't really think so. And where did you get all your money?"

She looked up at him, surprised. "Believe me, I've earned it."

Bear stopped, as if waiting for the right words to come to him. He looked away, and for a moment he saw his face reflected in the window. "What are you hiding, Jade? Why are you so secretive?"

"That's not true," she said. "I'm not secretive, just private."

A lie that begs for mercy, he thought. She's going to break soon. And he was eager to have it happen. Unless he knew it all, there was no future for them. But perhaps when that happened, there'd be nothing left to build on. He didn't know. But he had to find out.

"Why do you have to go snooping?" she demanded, starting for the kitchen door.

"Why the hell should you hide things from me?" Rising, Bear grabbed her by the shoulders. "Why?"

Jade looked up at him, narrowing her eyes. "Because you wouldn't understand the truth."

Bear believed that everyone has two memories. The one they can tell and the one that is stuck to the underside of that, the dark tarry smear of what really happened. He knew that Jade was taking a few extra minutes to answer his questions so that she could weigh and choose her words carefully. Her face was sometimes as clear as a photograph, and sometimes it faded and was suddenly gone, like chalk washed off the sidewalk.

"Why would my understanding matter to you?" Bear asked.

"You know why," she told him, in a voice that sounded as though someone had torn it into bits. "I've always loved you, Bear. There's never been another person."

Even in the half-light, he could see tiny smudges of shadows beneath her eyes that were not there a few

minutes ago. "You are the only woman I've ever loved.
I want you. But we cannot go forward, Jade, until there's
truth between us."

Bear sat down again and looked at her. "Tell me
everything." He felt pain pour over his shoulders, a pain
that came into his eyes. He was sorry for her, and for
himself—for everyone in the world who had suffered
when it was so unnecessary to suffer.

"Can we talk later?" she begged. She said it so softly, it
was as if she was actually down on her knees before him.

When she retreated into silence, he grew angrier.
This was like trying to fill a bucket of water with an
eyedropper. Was she employing some defensive strategy,
or was this all something left over from her childhood?

"All right,' Jade said in a determined rush. "But I've
done some terrible things in my life. At least, that may
be what you'll think, even though there was always a
good reason."

So, he told himself, the closet door was opening at
last, and as always, the skeletons were about to tumble
out.

"When I left Rochester a few months after you, I was
penniless, terrified, and friendless," Jade began. "I had
no one in the world to depend on besides myself. I've
worked hard, saved, done my best to put my past behind
me, but . . ." She broke off then, silent, staring into space
for half a minute, leaving the rest of her story hanging
between them.

Bear watched her as she spoke, gesturing strangely
in the air with one hand, then her hand subsided into
her lap again like a fallen bird. She seemed to struggle
physically to form the words. When finally they rushed
forth, they did so in spurts, her hands now clenched. He
hadn't anticipated his own grief, woven with the dark

threads of her past. Instinct told him that this would end badly.

He listened without making eye contact, staring off with a look of grave intent into the middle distance, nodding so she would know that he was taking in all that she was saying. The time of revelation, when all is known, although nothing is understood.

Bowing her head and in a soft voice, she told him everything, and despite the nausea that rose in his throat, he saw her bound up in her own chains, knowing that nothing, no force of law, or mercy, or public opinion, could save her.

She was always going to be a beautiful, but wounded woman, he thought. Had her fate been as inevitable as someone's with a dread disease whose future had already been buried in their genes the minute they were born? Had those demons been present at her birth? What had drawn him to her all those years ago? Of course, her vulnerability, but also their shared history. Both orphans. Both victims.

"You probably think I'm horrible," she concluded huskily, her eyes full of tears, "but I've always tried to do right, to live right, to help people where I could." She held back a sob, seemed to bite it down with a tremor along her jaw, and then inhaled deeply several times through flared nostrils.

Although he wondered if she had really told him everything, it was grievous to see the sadness he himself had authored. He felt his throat constrict—his passion for her and his rage running along the same edge—his brain reeling as the questions that he had been afraid to ask collided with answers he didn't want to hear. Leaning across the table, Bear tried to take her hand in his.

"Don't you touch me, *Detective Kuruk*," she cried, her neck corded with sudden rage. "You think you can just investigate me secretly like some ordinary criminal, and then test me to see if I'd tell the truth? You can get the hell out of my house. Get out," she shrilled when he followed her into the hallway, her hands making frantic waving gestures toward the door.

In that moment, she was a stranger to him.

"Why?" he shouted. "Are you going to kill me, too?" Her expression silenced him, and he shuddered at the unfairness of what he had just said—an unjustifiable cruelty.

Suddenly, she turned and moved in his direction. Her face was wild with betrayal, her eyes tiny beads. "Get out. Do you hear me?" Her fingers clenched into his upper arm, squeezing her nails into his flesh. "I should have realized I couldn't trust you. You're like everyone I have ever known. Except for Wendy. Go find who murdered her, Mr. Detective, and leave me alone."

Jerking open the door, Bear strode out of the house and into the searing heat of the day. Overhead, he could tell a storm was brewing, but the rolling clouds did nothing to cool the air. By the time he got to his car, he could feel sweat dripping down his back.

CHAPTER FORTY-SEVEN

Trembling, Jade stood in the doorway of Wendy's apartment. "I can do this," she said aloud. "I can do this." But the large black stain on the living room Oriental, the sight of it—Wendy's blood—pressed her back against the wall. *What kind of person would murder someone?*

Before their trip, Jade and Wendy had watched a sparrow build a nest on the window's ledge. Now Jade saw that she was sitting on her eggs. The little brown bird was, in an indefinable way, a comfort, a warmth that made it possible for her to go directly to the kitchen, where she took down two of Wendy's tea cups and saucers, and wrapped them in paper towels, after which she chose three sterling silver teaspoons—one for her retreat box—and placed them all carefully next to her handbag.

But the real reason she had come was to beg for forgiveness. How could she go on without it? Forgiveness for what, she wasn't sure, but it must have something to do with when she had gone back to talk to Wendy. In her disappointment and hurt, she might have said terrible things to her about abandonment or deceit. *Or lying about loving her.* Leaving things for her in a will didn't excuse the fact that she had encouraged Jade to love her, and then made plans to leave her. *"Goodbye, come visit us sometime."*

How could Wendy have done that to her, knowing what she did about all that Jade had lost already?

And there on the windowsill was the African violet that she had given Wendy last winter, thriving, unperturbed. Even flowers go on without you, so fierce was death.

Now that she had asked for Wendy's forgiveness, Jade hoped that, maybe, she could move ahead without her, provided Bear would be able to see her as a new person, just as he had done when he had banished Jadine by naming her Jade.

In some twisted way, Wendy had brought Bear back into Jade's life, a gift for which she would always be grateful. And that was, perhaps, the sign of forgiveness that Jade had hoped for.

It was all so strange, but she still couldn't remember what had actually transpired when she had returned to Wendy's apartment that night. Had she changed her mind about moving to Florida? If so, whatever had happened to Wendy was for nothing.

Not having spoken to Bear since he'd left her house, now Jade was holding her breath, waiting, hoping he would see that she was no longer that terrible person he must have thought she had become.

Choking back her sobs, Jade stood in Wendy's doorway for the last time.

Good-bye, my friend. You will never be far from my heart.

At home, Jade held the phonebook in her lap opened to *Auctioneer,* and arranged with the Skinner people to put up the entire contents of Wendy's apartment for auction, the proceeds to go to the Arnold Arboretum, the tranquil haven in Jamaica Plain where they had gone every season. It would, she thought, be a fitting memorial.

✲ ✲ ✲

The depression that had gripped Jade since Wendy had been so brutally murdered had returned the moment Bear had walked away, pulling her down in an undertow of despair. Why, why couldn't he have just left it alone? They could've just gone on from here. Made a new beginning. Why had she allowed him to trick her into revealing secrets that should have been kept hidden forever?

In the expanding rings of silence in which she sat, she heard a car door slam and footsteps on the walk. When the doorbell rang, she pulled Josie's afghan tight around her shoulders, sinking further into the couch. Whoever it was would go away.

But then, suddenly, Bear was standing over her, bellowing, "What am I supposed to do? Don't you see that there's nothing I can do to protect you? Nothing, goddammit."

Sweeping his hand through his hair, he groaned.

She sat up, staring at him, her heart pounding. His face was transformed by what she could only have described as anguish.

"I've sworn to uphold the law," he told her. "It's my obligation to tell the authorities everything you . . ." His voice broke off. Backing up, he stood against the doorway as though held there by a great force.

"Why, Bear?" she begged him. "Why do you need to tell anyone? Everything I told you about was in the past.

Besides, none of it was my fault. I didn't do anything wrong."

"You didn't do anything wrong?" He looked at her incredulously. Jade was afraid he was going to explode— or even hit her. "You killed your landlord, and then a man you didn't even know? That's not wrong?"

"It was self-defense, both times," she protested, her cheeks burning as if he had struck her with his hand instead of words. "I told you that. Would you prefer that they had murdered me?"

"What about the woman who adopted you, gave you her name, gave you this house? What is the matter with you, Jade, don't you have any conscience? How have you been able to live with yourself all these years?"

"Josie wouldn't have wanted to linger, I know that without a doubt. Her mind was gone, Bear. She was essentially a vegetable."

"What about Sophia," he persisted. "Did you really think you could play God like that?"

"She *wanted* me to give her the morphine. She made me promise." Jade suddenly felt disarmed and out of breath.

"You're a nurse, aren't you? You're supposed to *save* lives." He was pacing around the room, waving his arms like an evangelist preacher.

"Stop. Please stop." She raised her hands, palms out, as though to push the words away. "Anyway, it will never happen again. Bear, are you listening? I swear all that is in the past." She began to cry, her sobs filling the room like smoke. Without his weight holding her fast, she would be broken and scattered to the wind. She felt only terror that she would lose him again, and this time, forever.

"Can you ever forgive me?" A pleading note bent her voice. She hoped he could see, in her face, what her confession had cost her.

"It isn't me who needs to forgive you, Jade. You've broken the law. Over and over again. Don't you understand that you can't go unpunished?" He crossed over to the living room window, his back to her.

"So, I guess you hate me now." It was an accusation he couldn't allow to stand.

"No, Jade, I love you. I only hate what you have done."

He left her then, but in the days to come, rage rose in him that he could not control. Never before had he allowed his emotions to affect his performance as an officer, but those days were over now.

CHAPTER FORTY-EIGHT

"What did you say?" Bear snarled at the young man leaning against the chain-link fence.

"I said that I wasn't doing nothing bad," he replied. "Just talkin'."

"You make a habit of hanging around playgrounds and *talking* to eight-year-old boys?"

"No. Besides, there's no law against just talkin' to somebody."

"There is when you ask him for a blow job."

"I never did that. You're wrong. The kid was lying."

"You ever been arrested?" Lappas asked.

The young man didn't answer.

"Come on. Come on, we can check in a minute," Bear said, wildly impatient.

"Okay. Yes. I've been arrested before."

"How many times?"

"Twice."

"What for?"

"Some kid made a complaint." He took Bear's arm. "But neither time was true."

"You don't want to get any closer to me," Bear told him, "and you certainly don't want to lay that hand on me again."

"So, we've got a child molester here," Lappas said. "Big deal. Let's take him down to the station and book him. No need to fly off the handle."

But it was too late. Without warning, Bear crashed his fist into the side of the young man's head. It was a colossal blow that felled him to the ground where he lay moaning.

"For crissakes, Kuruk, back off," Lappas shouted, shoving Bear out of the way.

The wind whipped the dust into violent spirals, ripping through the playground. A jet flew over them, headed out from Logan, as Bear got into their Chevy and slumped far down on the seat, leaving the door open for the pent-up heat to escape. He was in agony. *What should he do? What in God's name should he do?* And he sure as hell wasn't thinking about the pervert who Lappas was escorting this way. His rage had everything to do with Jade. What kind of twisted thinking had allowed her to commit those terrible acts?

He punched the steering wheel.

His whole career had been about preventing crimes such as hers, and he knew that if he were able to accept her just the way she was, he would have to turn his back on everything he had lived by. Yet the pain of time lost between them was excruciating, and his cruelty toward her was now like a splinter, festering, the skin growing around it.

He let his head fall back against the leather seat and pinched the top of his nose hard to keep the tears from coming.

CHAPTER FORTY-NINE

Monday, and then Tuesday floated past her, leaving Jade yearning to be in a place where her life made sense. But where was that? She watched the tree limbs begin to shake as the wind picked up, throwing shadows of the branches through the window and across her lap. She sat so still that she felt she might simply disappear.

Would he actually turn her in? Would Bear do that to her—to them?

There had never been a rehearsal for such a conversation—her confession, the spilling out of actions that, when simply put into words, turned to poison. She still believed that if you did not actively *wish* to harm someone, then you have done them no harm, except, upon hearing herself talk about things that she had done, they had brought such horror to Bear's face. *What would he have wanted her to do?* Even so, she still believed that you can make tragic mistakes and still be a good person.

Jade went from the living room to the bedroom, dragging Josie's afghan up the stairs, needing it for comfort. Curling up on the bed, she pulled the pillow that Bear had used tight against her breast, breathing in his scent. No one knows what other people are capable of doing, or being, she thought. Maybe it's just as well. But he's a cop. He should know the forces that drive people to commit crimes.

Crimes. Was that what she had committed? No! Twice she had tried to defend herself and twice she had brought women she loved to peace. True crime is what happened to Wendy. Why wasn't Bear solving that instead of getting involved with what was, after all, ancient history now?

She had tried so hard, so very hard, and for so long, to become the woman she was. And yet she felt, now that she had told Bear everything, and had seen the look in his eyes, that she had no clear knowledge of herself anymore.

The sky had turned to pewter, and then the rain started—drops sliding down the bedroom window like tears that were too late in coming. Everything in life was change, she thought, except the past, and that must always remain as it had been. Those were memories she could only fold into her grief.

When she finally drifted off to sleep, the dreams she had known would come returned to haunt her— angry dreams in which people were sometimes shot. There was Mama, laughing, and now, there was Bear, laughing along with her. And no one felt her blows, no one registered the pitch of her screams. Once, when she awoke with a start, although she could not remember taking her retreat box from the drawer, she found herself clutching the stone that Bear had given her. *If only he would call.*

She couldn't help but acknowledge that those early years of Mama leaving, and Beaknose's rejection, and the "Aunties'" humiliation—the fetid years, as she thought of them—had damaged her irreparably. That must be what Bear thought, too—that she was damaged goods, and that no matter how hard she tried to justify the things she had done, in his eyes she was guilty.

In that instant, Jade came to the devastating realization that all of the important events of her life had already happened.

CHAPTER FIFTY

"Hey, what's going on with you and the girlfriend?" Lappas asked.

"She's still mourning her friend," Bear muttered.

"And you're cooling it for a while. Probably a good idea," Lappas told him. "So, do you think the Sox are ever going to get it together? Maybe just one more World Series in my lifetime?"

"Yeah." Bear wished that his partner didn't always think he needed to fill in conversational gaps. He had grown to like Lappas with his ponytail and five o'clock shadow. There was compatibility between them, a precise matching of opposites, but he wished Lappas would shut the hell up at times.

Hit with a wave of weariness after seventy-two hours without sleep, Bear's eyes stung with fatigue, and yet, the weariness brought with it an unexpected clarity. By confessing, Jade had allowed him to peer into her soul, at what lay broken and shattered there, like glittering glass. Knowing that he was strong enough to save her, he had decided *not* to initiate legal action that could destroy Jade and thereby him. He hadn't been prepared for the incredible feeling of relief that followed, as though a thousand pounds of weight had been lifted off his shoulders. He believed Jade when she had said that she would never again do what she had done in the past. *He could live with that, and was anxious now to let her know . . . to reassure her.* He regretted threatening her. After all these years alone, he knew now that he could not live without her, and having made the decision to protect her, he felt a euphoric sense of inner peace, unlike anything he had ever experienced, sweep over him.

"Robbery in progress," Yvonne announced calmly over the speaker, cutting into Bear's thoughts. "118 Dartmouth Street. Neighbor heard screaming. Apartment 10C, fourth floor."

Although the day was slipping toward evening, the two detectives didn't discuss a plan. They didn't need to. In the years that they had been partners, they had grown used to working together as though they were one, anticipating each other's moves and approach to each new crime.

When the alert came in, they had just passed through the Big Dig, Boston's scandalous construction site smack in the middle of town.

"Call for backup," Bear told his partner as he tore down Commonwealth Ave. and took a right on Dartmouth, where he double-parked, jumped out of the car, and slapped a blue light on the roof.

The doorman frantically waved them through the revolving door. Ignoring the elevator inside the lobby, the two detectives ran up the stairs to the fourth floor. They could see that they were the first responders.

"Are you the police?" an elderly man, who was standing in the hallway, asked them.

"I'm one of them," Bear, breathing heavily, flipped out his shield. "Kuruk. Homicide. That's my partner, Lappas. Go back to your apartment and lock the door."

The two detectives paused on either side of 10C. The door was slightly open. Bear could see that it had been forced. They stood listening a moment before Bear went in first, gun up, both scanning the room left and right, providing an overlapping field of fire. Almost immediately after entering the apartment, they saw a man lying on the floor, his hair matted with blood, partially concealing his shattered face. There was no time to think; hardly time to breathe.

"Police!" Bear shouted out. "Put your weapon down and come out with your hands in full view."

Moving swiftly across the room, he raised his gun, forefinger inside the trigger guard, thumb snapping off the safety, gun leveled toward the doorway.

"Behind you," Lappas shouted. There was a sudden explosion. Too late, Bear realized that the shot had come from a gun that was shockingly close—the acrid smell of it rushed to his nostrils.

A man in a black hooded sweatshirt, who was making a dash for the door, turned, and got off another shot. Lappas shifted his stance, and then, wide-legged and fierce, aimed carefully and deliberately. His gun bucked in his hand when he squeezed the trigger. The intruder clutched his leg and then stumbled toward the open doorway. Two more shots exploded, leaving behind them a room in which smoke hung in heavy layers in the air, and the stink of cordite.

Lappas knelt beside his partner who lay motionless, his blood spilling on the parquet floor. Checking his pulse, he then listened to the beats of his heart.

"Officer down," he shouted into his cell, and then, bending over Bear, heard him mutter, "Tell her . . . forgiven . . . Jade . . ."

Placing both hands on his partner's chest, Lappas began CPR; keeping it up until his arm became numb.

"Please don't do this, Kuruk. It's not your time." He followed one enormous thrust on his chest after another. "Come on, partner, I need you."

He continued until, thankfully, the EMTs came rushing into the room.

CHAPTER FIFTY-ONE

J ade was working in the backyard preparing the flowerbeds for winter when Lappas came around the side of the house, calling her name. She visored her hand to her forehead, blocking the sun from her eyes, and for a moment her hopes rose that it was Bear. Walking toward him, she stopped abruptly when she realized it was Lappas with a Red Sox jersey and a baseball cap turned backwards.

"What's the matter?" she demanded anxiously when she saw his face, white and hollow-cheeked. "What's happened?" she asked much louder. "Where is Bear?" Her heart began to beat erratically as she closed the space between them. Overhead, the pale sun burned without heat. The day was slowly tilting toward dusk.

"You need to come with me," he told her abruptly. "Bear's been shot." The man's shadow pooled at his feet, a dark stain in which he stood.

Wordlessly, she started running toward Lappas' car, throwing her trowel behind her. *Oh, God, oh, God . Please, not now. Don't let him die.*

As he drove, hunched over the wheel, Lappas repeated his partner's message: "Bear was saying something before he went unconscious. It was a message for you, Jade. Like he forgave you, or something like that."

"What was it exactly?"

"It sounded like, '*Tell Jade I forgive her.*' I don't know. For God's sake, it's all a blur."

"Okay. Thank you. Thank you." She sat on the front seat, rocking back and forth, her eyes closed, a strand of hair from her ponytail in her mouth.

When Jade and Lappas rushed into the emergency room, they found Bear lying on a gurney, pale and gaunt; the pulse monitor beeping incessantly; antibiotics dripping into his arm. The rubber-soled shoes of the nurses and doctors who surrounded him squeaked on the blood-stained linoleum floor. It was routine to them—patients choking their way back and forth along the border of life and death. But for Lappas and Jade, it was a nightmare.

Weaving her way between doctors, Jade took hold of Bear's hand, her nails still filled with dirt from the garden.

"Family?" a nurse asked, looking up at her, and Jade simply nodded. She was so much more to this man than "family," but they would never understand.

Looking around helplessly, Jade saw a young woman, her fist pressed against her mouth, and knew that it must be Yvonne. A doctor was speaking to Lappas, who stared at the floor, shaking his head in wide sweeps from side to side.

With fear pulsing through her veins, Jade walked over to him, and touched his arm. "What did he say to you?" she asked.

"Paralyzed from the chest down," Lappas said, avoiding her eyes. "The fucker got him in the back."

Jade rushed down the hall to the rest room. She turned on the cold faucet, filling the sink—her reflection tilted in the water, the eyes that watched her eyes. Scooping water into her palms, she pressed them against her forehead, her muscles stiffened.

So there it was. She could feel a change sweeping through her. It was as though she had managed to escape from some evil force, only to be caught by it from behind and dragged back into the darkness. She had thought she finally had a chance to seize a bit of happiness, and now, as always, it had been snatched away from her.

Except that Bear had forgiven her. It was a gift.

She would cling to that.

And she would care for him, as she had all the others.

CHAPTER FIFTY-TWO

"Recovery from a spinal cord injury is long and difficult, as well as intensely emotional. You have to be patient, and pray," all of the doctors and nurses had told her. But, of course, there *is* no such thing as recovery from a spinal cord injury. Jade knew that, and so did everyone else. No more being a Boston Homicide Detective, no more running six miles in the early morning or climbing mountains, no more making love to Jade . . . *But he could still love her.*

Outside the hospital window, maple leaves shimmered gold in the early fall sunlight, an insult now rather than a joy when she remembered so clearly that day on Monadnock. If only she could reverse the clock, be with Bear again on top of the mountain, and then have time stop. Have the world end.

Within hours of the shooting, they had operated on Bear, attempting to take pressure off the injured spinal cord, hoping against hope that this would allow *some* neurological function to occur. In the following two weeks, while they waited to see what would happen, Jade lived adrift in shadows, spending night and day by his bedside, going home only to shower and change clothes. Lappas and Yvonne were there every chance they could, and Jade was thankful for their support, but not their pity. Bear would hate that.

Often, after Lappas left, Yvonne would offer to stay with Jade, but she sent her away since there could never be anything even resembling a friendship when her soul was held down by an unmovable stone.

At first, Bear was induced into a deep sleep, but by the fourth week they started to bring him out of it. A doctor hurried past her, stethoscope draped around his neck like a sacred snake, not unlike the kind that Jade dreamed about. Was he avoiding her? Was it the worst kind of news? Lappas and Yvonne joined her so that they could be there the minute Bear opened his eyes. Waiting, she felt like someone playing a role she did not really understand. Words came to mind, and then just congealed in her throat.

When finally Bear's eyes fluttered open, he said hoarsely, "Did we get that bastard?"

"He's dead," was Lappas' reply, the features of his face as misaligned as though they had been re-carved by an inept sculptor.

Bear must have seen it, too. He had gone still, listening intently, alert to the altered tones and cadences of their voices. Or perhaps he'd tried to move and discovered the truth.

"What's happened to me?" he gasped. His voice broke off as if it had no place to go.

Struggling to frame a reply, to give him an answer that would not destroy him, Jade tested the art of subterfuge, determined to tell him the truth and still leave him with hope.

"There's been spinal trauma, Bear," she told him, "but the doctor operated to ease back the pressure on the nerves and . . ."

His expression was that of a mountaineer's at the moment when his rope snapped. A savage groan ripped through his throat. "I'm paralyzed? Oh, God, I can't feel my legs."

"But Bear," Yvonne broke in, "they think the nerves that go to your arms and hands have been spared. In terms of sensation and motor function, that is . . ." She stopped speaking when she realized what she was saying, and to whom she was saying it.

He gasped and coughed, tears standing in his eyes. "No!" was all he screamed when he could speak again.

Then Jade took over, searching for a possibility that would give him something to cling to.

"There is stem cell research, transplant potential, promising developments . . ."

Her voice ran down like the alarm of a wind-up clock. *How can someone who has a thirst for action possibly endure the absence of it?*

"Leave me alone! All of you," Bear told them in an ominously quiet voice, and when her eyes met his, Jade knew that, in the face of his determination, they had no choice but to do exactly what he said.

CHAPTER FIFTY-THREE

Six weeks later, Bear was brought from rehab to Jade's house by ambulance. It had begun to snow that morning. Tiny needle-like crystals blown by a bitter wind, lashed at Bear as they carried him into the house. Positioned where the morning sun would come early through the east window, no matter how pale, Jade had transformed the living room with a hospital bed that had pulley bars attached so Bear could help maneuver himself if he built enough strength for it, and she had placed the TV so he could watch it comfortably. There were fresh flowers on the side table.

The operation on Bear's spine had accomplished nothing as far as his ability to use his legs, and very little for his arms and hands. There was some movement there, but he was still so weak. Jade had listened carefully to the directions for what she was to do at home to continue building strength in his upper extremities, but when she was told his muscles had already begun to atrophy—that rehab had accomplished so little—she felt distraught.

"Please, close the curtain, the sun hurts my eyes," was the first thing Bear said to Jade once he was settled and they were alone. "And take those flowers away. The smell makes me nauseous." Immediately, he retreated into stillness, snatching his senses inwards, away from the surface of his skin, into some deeper more inaccessible recess. His intractable silences struck Jade to the core.

Nothing she did made him the least bit happy, and he refused to even try the exercises with her. For days, he just drifted, indifferent, into a solitude that gradually engulfed them both. At intervals, Jade put on her coat and boots, clomped down the slippery back porch steps, and picked her way through the crusted snow to the purple smoke tree. There, in the bleak winter landscape, the wind sharp in her hair, she sobbed aloud and unheard, railing against God, or fate, or luck—whatever had allowed this tragedy to enter her life.

At night, Jade slept beside him in Josie's old lounge chair, in case he might need her. It was impossible for her to eat. She felt depleted, almost faint. She had not anticipated that her grief and anger would match his own. How, she asked herself, could she live without Bear?

One evening, weeks after leaving the hospital, they were lying next to each other, their disembodied voices rising in the darkened room. Bear's voice began to tentatively reach across the space between them.

"I can't live like this, Jade," he said.

The thin persistent wail of the teakettle whistling in the kitchen filled the room. She turned on a light by the bed. He flinched, and closed his eyes.

"If only you would try the exercises . . ."

"You *know* what I mean," he said, no longer sounding angry.

He was pleading.

They exchanged a look that connected them in a way that excluded everything else as she shared his longing and despair, and Jade knew that she was looking into his very soul.

"I want to be in a place where the truth isn't true any longer," he implored her, "a place where there will be no more struggle."

In that moment, Jade knew that something had been stripped away. Stumbling to the closet, she took down her retreat box, and making her way to the kitchen, she dropped it into the trashcan and then poured the boiling water down the kitchen sink, feeling the steam rise to her face.

Wendy had *not* forgiven her. None of them had.

When she finally had the strength to face him, his expression nearly tore her heart in two.

"I understand," was all she said, when a sob like none she had ever heard before broke from his chest.

"I'll do anything you want me to." Her throat ached. Slowly, she saw him relax into the darkness, letting her promise move through him in waves.

CHAPTER FIFTY-FOUR

At first, she felt a sense of panic at what she had agreed to do. But as soon as the decision was made, time took on a curiously practical quality. There were certain legal details to be taken care of. After that, everything else became unimportant.

Bear wanted to leave his money to The Home in Rochester. It had, he told Jade, made him the person he had become—a man who regretted nothing about the way he had conducted his life.

As for Jade, her real start in life had come much later, long after the "Aunties" had done their worst. Cheryl had been the first person to believe in her potential and had given her a chance to succeed. So it was that she decided to endow Serene Haven Nursing Home with everything that she was about to leave behind.

On the way back from the lawyer and the drugstore, Jade passed a graveyard; a cluster of thin, blackened headstones, encircled by a wrought iron fence, plastic flowers sticking up through drifts of snow—the field beyond, a winter desert. She felt glad that their ashes would be strewn from the top of Monadnock on a windy day.

Everything was taken care of.

Moving Bear over to the edge of the hospital bed in order to make room for herself, Jade nestled against him, lacing her fingers through his, knowing that that was the only touch he could feel, and that he would understand that it was time and that nothing more needed to be said.

It was deep dusk outside; the lights of the neighboring houses came on like evening stars. The wind was relentless. Shutters creaked.

Crystals glistened under porch lights. The town shimmered, luminescent.

The streets were silenced, lined with drifts like frozen waves; a theater of white.

Ice glazed every yard—turned gravel to diamonds, garbage to ransoms.

The midnight sky hung over it all, like a blue stone.

And the quiet that settled over Josie's house was like a blessing.

END

✿ ✿ ✿

READING GROUP GUIDE

Questions for Discussion

1. Jade is certainly a psychologically damaged human being. But what are her strengths? How does the author make her a likeable character?

2. How do you think Jade's childhood predetermined her inclination to violence as an adult? How did Bear's childhood affect him?

3. What do you think of the "Aunties" of Rochester? What is the author saying about the dangers of false charity? In her attraction to older women, was Jade acting on true charity, yearning for a mother figure, or was it strictly a means of obtaining emotional security for herself?

4. If you were confronted as Jade was by her landlord or by the man in the hotel, would you have reacted as she did? What kind of reasoning allowed Jade to tell Bear that she did nothing wrong? As you read, did you think of her as a murderess?

5. Do you find Jade's euthanasia or "mercy killings" of Josie and Sophia any more or less acceptable than the "self-defense" killings? Do you think murder is ever morally right?

6. What do you think happened when Jade went back to Wendy's apartment? Why does she seem not to remember what transpired there?

7. Upon discovering Sophia's body, Lappas said, "Suicide is the easy way out and usually packs a message: *see how I love you,* or, *see what you made me do.*" "Maybe," Bear told him, "but as I see it, suicide is anger, coupled with despair." Did you see this exchange as foreshadowing the ending?

8. What other ending do you think would have suited this story?

CPSIA information can be obtained at www.ICGtesting.com
Printed in the USA
BVOW08s1944020813

327707BV00012B/196/P

9 781451 597776